Fried Catfish

M.C. Madjoucoff

First Stillwater River Publications Edition

ISBN: 978-1-952521-77-5

1 2 3 4 5 6 7 8 9 10
Written by M.C. Madjoucoff
Published by Stillwater River Publications,
Pawtucket, RI, USA.

Publisher's Cataloging-In-Publication Data
(Prepared by The Donohue Group, Inc.)

Names: Madjoucoff, M. C., author.
Title: Fried catfish / M.C. Madjoucoff.
Description: First Stillwater River Publications edition. |
Pawtucket, RI, USA : Stillwater River Publications, [2021]
Identifiers: ISBN 9781952521775
Subjects: LCSH: Divorced women--Middle West--Drama. |
Online dating--Drama. | Computer crimes--Drama. |
Undercover operations--Malta--Drama. | LCGFT: Screenplays.
Classification: LCC PS3613.A2848 F75 2021 |
DDC 813/.6--dc23

This book is dedicated to my Mom,
who brought laughter into my life and
who has always been there for me
when I needed her.

Contents

SCENE 1

MALTA: INTERNET WEB CAFÉ/OFFICE—MID-MORNING

[ABEL: *A young dark-skinned man, mid-20s, nose too big for his face, dark eyes and hair. He is slim, has a cocky look, wears name brand clothes and sneakers and is unshaven. He speaks French. He also goes by the online name "Stefan."*]

ABEL: [*sitting at his desk, rocking his chair back and forth, starting to type something while he is on a phone call with a headset*]

Hey baby! How is my darling girl today?

[*turning his head to his left, he winks at his male co-worker*]

[*with a soft deep voice*]

Yeess baaybee, I miss you too! I looovvveee you! I can't wait to see you. [*kissing sounds*]

[*looking at an image of dating website profile of a woman in her early 50s, he sticks his finger in his throat and mimes vomiting*]

Baby? Did you send me the $4,000 yet? All I need is this and it will allow me to get my passport back and buy my plane ticket to see you.

Okay... honey... that's great baby! I love you! I will look at my account and call you later. Byyyeee!

[*kissing sounds*]

[CALL ENDS]

ABEL: [*turning to his male coworker again*]

...and that's how it's done!

[*bangs his fist on the desk*]

[*A FEMALE MANAGER—she is elegant, tall, dressed for business, high heels—hair pulled back in pony-tail with glasses. She walks to ABEL's desk and stands behind his chair.*]

FEMALE MANAGER: [*in French—in a harsh tone*]

Did you get the money?

ABEL: [*in French, with a coy look*]

But of course my dear.

FEMALE MANAGER: [*in French, with disdain*]

Cut the crap and show me the money, you idiot!

ABEL: [*in French, becomes more serious*]

Hey is that any way to talk to your top producer?

[*types furiously and displays a bank account online, points to the amount of $4,000 USD*]

SCENE 1

[*in French with enthusiasm*]

There! There is the money!

FEMALE MANAGER: [*in French, with disinterested tone*]

Good! Okay… dump her! On to the next victim.

[FEMALE MANAGER *walks away.*]

ABEL: [*in French under his breath*]

Bitch!

END SCENE

SCENE 2

WISCONSIN, U.S.A. SUBURBS— ONE FAMILY HOME—
OUTSIDE—SUNNY—SEPTEMBER—FALL-LIKE WEATHER—
9:30AM—DAUGHTER SARA GOES TO COLLEGE

[*Eldest daughter* SARA *(a pretty blond, blue eyes, average size, approximately* LAURIE's *height) is moving to college. The trunk of her SUV is open in the driveway and she is finishing placing items in and ready to close the door.*
   LAURIE (MAIN CHARACTER): *A middle-aged white woman, mid-length light brown hair, green eyes, a bit overweight, dresses nicely, no taller than 5'6.*]

[LAURIE *walks to the car holding a taped up box, handing the box to her daughter.*]

LAURIE: OKAY honey… here ya' go.

   [*with a sad face*] That should be the last of it. You make sure you call me when you get there!

SARA: [*taking box out of* LAURIE's *hands*]

   Oh, MOM, I will only be an hour away! Don't make me feel bad about leaving you and I will be back for the rehearsal dinner in a few weeks.

   [SARA *places the box in the trunk—she turns back to her mom and they hug.*]

LAURIE: [*still hugging*] I know, I know, but you

4

SCENE 2

are my baby and I will always worry about you!

[SARA's *sister CARA (A pretty girl, brownish hair, green eyes, slim, little taller than LAURIE) comes up behind them both and they have a group hug.*]

LAURIE: [*smiling*] Well at least I still have one of my babies here with me…

[*They separate.*]

SARA: [*turns to her sister and hugs her*] Okay, Sis—I'll text you later. Take care of Mom will ya'?

CARA: Of course!

[SARA *gets in the car, starts it, slowly drives off with her hand waving from the open window and beeps. LAURIE and CARA stand side by side, arms around each other, heads touching, and both wave goodbye.*]

CARA: Mom, I'm going to Tiffany's house, I'll be home for dinner.

[*She kisses LAURIE—walks down the driveway and away from view.*]

LAURIE: Okay, Kitkat, I'll see you later…

[*loudly with hands cupped on her mouth*] Pork chops and applesauce tonight!

END SCENE

SCENE 3

LAURIE'S HOME—INSIDE —SHORTLY AFTER
SARA LEAVES—DRIVEWAY SCENE

[LAURIE *goes in the house, closes the door, stands behind it for about 30 seconds while breathing and deeply sighs. She can't believe one of her daughters has just gone off to college.*]

LAURIE: [*to herself*] You got this! You can handle it Laurie!

[LAURIE *walks by pictures of her and her daughters hanging on the wall and smiles.*]

FLASHBACK

[*She feels nostalgic, images of when her kids were younger, little things like baking cookies, making a snowman, visualizing her and her ex-husband sitting on their couch holding hands, kissing and remembering how happy she was.*
   Visions of her arguing with her ex—then seeing "Final Divorce" paper in her face.]

LAURIE: [*shaking her head*]

Where did it all go?

What happened to love?

What happened to me?

I miss LOVE! ROMANCE!

SCENE 3

[*putting both hands over her eyes, then looking up screams*]

GOD, WHERE'S MY TRUE LOVE?

[*She walks to the next room.*]

[LAURIE *is now in her little spare room, and signs on to her laptop computer. She signs on to her online banking and accesses her bank account. It shows approximately $15,000 in her checking account.*

LAURIE *pays some of her bills. She leans back and put her hands over her eyes to rub them. She then checks her email.*

LAURIE *reads an email invitation to join an online dating site called "Catch your Mate." She views some pics and sees there are a lot of good looking men with their shirts off, buff and muscular.*]

LAURIE: [*under her breath*]

Yeah, right—like this guy would be interested in me.

[*One of the lines reads, "Looking for your true love?" LAURIE takes this as a sign. She just finished saying the same words.*

She starts to fill out the basic info for her online profile. She uploads a nice picture of herself from a trip she took with her kids. The website asks for a credit card, and she pauses.]

LAURIE: [*to herself*]

Do I really want to do this? Spend money on this?

7

Who am I kidding? These guys on here want some twenty-something, not a divorce' with adult kids.

[*She gets a little down. Closes her laptop and walks to the kitchen. LAURIE continues on with her day.*

LAURIE is now in the kitchen, her cellphone rings. Caller ID shows—MOM.]

LAURIE: [*with enthusiasm*]

Hi Mom! How are you doing?

Oh yeah—I almost forgot about that! I'll pick you up in 15 minutes… see you in a few.

[LAURIE *grabs her keys from the kitchen counter and her purse, locks the door and gets into her car.*]

END SCENE

SCENE 4

SPENDING TIME WITH MOM AT THE FARMER'S MARKET.
LAURIE LEAVES HER HOUSE—OUTSIDE SAME DAY—LATER TIME.

[LAURIE *backs out of the driveway—driving down the street—puts the radio on—she loves 80's/90's music. She is listening to an 80's song. Her car window is down—while driving she starts lip synching. She comes to a stoplight. Another car comes along her driver's side and three college-age kids in a another car all look at her, watching her sing the song currently playing on the radio.*]

COLLEGE KID 1: Yeah, maybe you should go back— waaay back to 1980! I wasn't even born then!

COLLEGE KIDS: Ha, ha, ha!

[*The light turns green, college kids' car speeds off.*]

LAURIE: [*under her breath*]

I wish I could go back—things were so much easier back then!

[*She arrives at her mother's street and pulls in her driveway. LAURIE's MOM—Renee (A woman in her seventies, short and resembles LAURIE in figure. Short dirty blond hair, dresses in Bohemian outfits. Very easygoing.)*
She is just stepping out her door with her purse in hand and locking her front door. She turns around and walks toward the car. She gets in the passenger side door and plops herself down and

closes the door. Turning to her daughter, she hugs her.]

MOM: Hey there lovely girl, how's my best girl today?! Ready to go to the Farmer's Market?!

LAURIE: Yes Mom—Ready!

[LAURIE *starts the car, and they drive off to their destination.*]

MOM: What's the matter honeypot?

LAURIE: Mom, you know that I am okay with Dan getting remarried right?

MOM: Right.

LAURIE: Well, actually I have been feeling sad and empty since I found out Dan was getting remarried, and with Sara moving to college now it's just a matter of time before Cara leaves me too. I haven't been dating, I don't have anyone in my life who I love and who loves me.

MOM: What are you talking about? I love you! Sara and Cara love you! What's going on? You sound like you're feeling sorry for yourself.

LAURIE: Maybe I do… Sara and Cara don't need me anymore.

[*emphatically*]

They have a better social life than I do!

MOM: Well, we are going to do something about that! I am going to take you to my senior center and you are going to learn salsa dancing! [*she starts chair dancing*]

LAURIE: Mom! Senior center?! Really—how old do you think I am?

MOM: You are only as old as you feel, and you should see some of the good looking men that belong there. There are two men that we dance with on a regular basis: Jack and Harry. Jack had his hip replaced and that has done wonders for getting his legs in the right spot.

LAURIE: Okay Mom, T.M.I.! I don't want to hear that about my mom! What would Dad say?

MOM: Well, if your dad was still alive, I'm sure he wouldn't like it, but, now that he's gone—I am sure he is looking down on me and saying "Reneé you still got the moves."

LAURIE: Ok, now that's enough! Keep stories about you and Dad's intimate details to yourself.

MOM: Oh, come on Laurie, don't be such a prude! I thought you and I could have these conversations someday. We all need to live a little! Hashtag YOLO!

LAURIE: YOLO? What does that mean?

MOM: "You Only Live Once," that's my new slogan!

LAURIE: Oh, great! Even my own mom is hipper than me!

[*They arrive at the farmer's market. It's in a large park. They both exit the vehicle and start walking toward it. They pass a vendor selling fruit. MOM picks up a peach and smells it and then puts in front of LAURIE's nose.*]

MOM: Smell that! It's sweet!

[MOM *puts the peach back.*]

LAURIE: [*sarcastically*]

Sweet you say—I scream, you scream, we all scream for ice cream!

MOM: Ice cream! Ooh, that sounds great actually!

[MOM *spots an ice cream truck and starts walking toward it.*]

MOM: Come Laurie—pick your favorite cone!

[LAURIE *follows her.*]

MOM: Remember how you used to feel better after you had an ice cream cone!

[*They both get to the VENDOR's window, no one else is there. Salsa music is playing on his radio. MOM starts dancing salsa while the VENDOR is watching.*]

LAURIE: [*looking embarrassed and with pursed lips*]

Mom, STOP THAT! You're embarrassing us!

MOM: I'm not embarrassed! Lighten up Laurie! You

are too uptight! [*still dancing*] Loosen up! Here take my hand.

LAURIE: No Mom, come on, STOP, PLEASE!

[ICE CREAM VENDOR *is watching them and dancing in his truck, smiling.* LAURIE *starts to loosen up—dances a little with her* MOM.]

MOM: [*smiling*] See… now that wasn't so bad!

LAURIE: [*smiling*] Yeah, Mom, I guess not.

[*They both dance up to the truck window to place their orders.*]

MOM: [*with slight Spanish accent asks* LAURIE] Okay *señorita*, what will it be?

LAURIE: A small cone with vanilla… please.

MOM: Ok, sir—we will have a plain old boring vanilla and give me a large waffle cone with kahlua coffee ice cream… please,

[*turning to* LAURIE] That's what you need! A little flavor in your life! Spice things up a bit! We should go shopping and buy some lingerie. Maybe we can get a good photographer to take a nice picture of you.

LAURIE: Mom, it sounds like you haven't heard a word I said. I want someone to love me for ME! Not what they think I am or can be.

MOM: I've listened… I just think you need to

think outside the box. Go for a guy that you wouldn't have gone for before. You are an amazing woman and you deserve to be happy.

[*The* ICE CREAM VENDOR *hands them the ice cream cones.*]

MOM: [*handing the* VENDOR *the money*] Keep the change my dear!

ICE CREAM VENDOR: [*Spanish accent*] Anything else I can do for you ladies [*he winks at* LAURIE] let me know.

LAURIE: [*turns and looks at* MOM *with a wry smile, eyebrows up*] No thanks, the ice cream will do.

ICE CREAM VENDOR: OKAY BABY! [*rings his bell*]

[*They start walking away from the truck.*]

MOM: [*licking ice cream cone*] See there, he liked you. Why not flirt a little?

LAURIE: With an ice cream truck vendor, OKAY Mom! Thanks for the dating advice Mom.

MOM: Just trying to help.

[*Time passes. They leave the farmers' market, go back in the car, end up back at* MOM's *driveway.*]

LAURIE: Thanks for today Mom, I had a great day, and thanks for listening!

SCENE 4

MOM: Of course sugar plum! That's what I am here for. I love you!

[*They hug in the car. MOM gets out of the car, closes the door. Passenger window is down.*]

LAURIE: I love you too Mom!

[MOM *starts walking to her door, doing a little salsa dancing as she goes. We only see her back. She raises her arm to wave goodbye!*]

[LAURIE *makes a face as she sees her mother, shakes her head, and drives off*]

END SCENE

SCENE 5

LAURIE'S HOUSE—SMALL SPARE ROOM WHERE SHE KEEPS HER COMPUTER—IT'S AFTER 7:00 P.M.—DARK OUTSIDE. SHE GRABS HERSELF A GLASS OF WINE. SHE IS CHECKING HER EMAILS. SHE SEES THAT SHE HAS GOTTEN A FEW LIKES AND ONE MESSAGE ON HER DATING WEBSITE PROFILE.

LAURIE: [*surprised look on her face*] A message? ...Huh! But, I can't read it of course until I pay to join. Oh well, just for the entertainment, let me see who sent me a message.

[LAURIE *goes to the kitchen, opens her purse, takes out a credit card, goes back to her computer.*]

LAURIE: [*starts typing her credit card info*]

Okay, here we go!

[LAURIE *opens up the only email she received, sees the profile pic for a man named* STEFAN—*it's a very good looking man in his mid to late 40s with a few pics: him fishing, with a dog, with a young boy, alone.*]

LAURIE: [*eyes widen with surprise*]

Wow! He's handsome!

[*She starts reading. While reading she puts her hand on her heart and looks enchanted with his words*]

[Email from STEFAN to LAURIE] Dear Beautiful Lady,

16

I hope this email finds you well! I had to write to you to tell you how I enjoyed reading your profile. You have beautiful soulful eyes. They have caught my attention and I can't stop thinking about them. I am a God fearing man and I pray that you will write me back. With blessings. Stefan

LAURIE: That is so sweet!

[*She decides to write him back feeling inspired by his words*]

[Email from LAURIE to STEFAN] Hello Stefan. Thank you—yes, I am well. I hope you are too! Thank you for your compliments! I think you are very handsome and would like to know more about you. Laurie

[*Approximately one hour goes by and* LAURIE *sees she received a new email from* STEFAN. *She gets excited. They email back and forth for a few hours.*]

[Email from STEFAN to LAURIE] Hello Again My Dear! Of course, I am so blessed that you write back to me. I Thank God to receive an email from your beautiful soul. I am an engineer by trade. A widower of 2 years. My wife die from cancer. I have a son. He is now 10. It has been hard for me raising him alone. I speak French. I travel a lot for my work. I await your next email. Stefan

[Email from LAURIE to STEFAN] Dear Stefan, I am so sorry to hear about your wife. That must be so hard for you to raise a child alone. I

know, I have two daughters and I am divorced.
Laurie

[**Email from STEFAN to LAURIE**] I knew by looking
at your picture you were suffering like me.
Your beautiful eyes look so sad. I could feel
we had a connection. God has sent you to me.
Tell me, Laurie, what are you looking for in
a man? I want to know, tell me… Stefan

LAURIE: [*to herself*] Wow—he's deep and sensitive.

[**Email from LAURIE to STEFAN**] Stefan, I haven't
met a man like you before. So deep and direct.
I am looking for a man who will love me for
me. Look past my looks and my flaws and just
love me and be with me through thick and
thin. Laurie

[**Email from STEFAN to LAURIE**] Beautiful Laurie,
I am the man who can make your dreams come
true. I need you to know something. You are
beautiful. Your face, your eyes, they speak
to my heart, my soul. To know that you were
hurt by a man you loved makes me angry. How
can anyone treat you like that? If you allow
me, I can take your pain of this away. Let me
be your protector. Stefan

[**Email from LAURIE to STEFAN**] Dear Stefan, you don't
know me. How can you say such nice things to
me? I don't think you are real. Laurie

[**Email from STEFAN to LAURIE**] Darling Laurie, I
am real. I am all man. I know you because I
pray to God and asked him to send you to me.

SCENE 5

[A mushy e-card opens on screen and begins to play music. LAURIE *is engrossed with it.]*

> Please Laurie, believe me—I will show you I am real. I will prove it to you if you allow me.
>
> Stefan

[Email from LAURIE to STEFAN] Ok, Stefan, *[skeptical expression on her face as she types]* I believe you. I just never had a man talk to me like you. You are so handsome—so successful—I am surprised you would feel that way about me. I would like to know you better.

Laurie

[Email from STEFAN to LAURIE] Baby, you are too hard on yourself! I find your beauty in your eyes, in your soul. You have been hurt, man is evil, they don't see real beauty, I do!

Laurie, can I share something with you—don't think me foolish. Do you believe in love at first sight? I am falling in love you with you. I want to call you, to hear your voice. Can I call you?

Stefan

[Email from LAURIE to STEFAN] My phone number is: 414-495-4975

*[*LAURIE's *phone rings; she notices it is not an in-state number. She answers with hesitation.]*

FRIED CATFISH

LAURIE: Hello?

STEFAN: [*with French/African accent*]

   Hello baby, it's Stefan.

LAURIE: Hi!

   [*with excitement*]

   Nice to hear your voice!

STEFAN: Yours too baby!

LAURIE: So where are you? Where do you live?

STEFAN: I live in the United States, but I am in
   Italy now.

LAURIE: Italy?

STEFAN: Yes dear! My company flew me here to work
   on a bridge. I told you, I am an engineer.

LAURIE: Oh, wow! How long will you be there?

STEFAN: Another week or so.

LAURIE: Where do you live in the US?

STEFAN: I live in Chicago.

LAURIE: Illinois! That is one state away from me!

STEFAN: Where are you dear?

SCENE 5

LAURIE: Wisconsin!

STEFAN: I have visited there before. See I knew we were meant to be, God is great!

LAURIE: Yeah, I guess so—small world.

STEFAN: Sweetie, I've got to go, my boss is calling me. Can I call you tomorrow?

LAURIE: Oh sure, please!

STEFAN: Okay, baby—I love you!

LAURIE: Stefan, I don't want to go that fast. [*embarrassed*] We just started talking, how can you say that? We haven't met yet.

STEFAN: I understand. You need to trust Laurie. I know you are a beautiful lady and you make me feel all warm inside. I am a patient man. I can wait for your love.

LAURIE: Oh wow! [*feeling warm and fuzzy inside*]

No one has ever said that to me before.

OKAY, have a good night!

STEFAN: Well get used to my love Laurie, I am going to bring you the world!

Good night baby, sweet dreams!

CALL ENDS

[It's late… LAURIE *can't get over the fact that such a good-looking man just called her and told her that he loves her. This is exactly what she has been waiting for since her divorce.*]

[*She thinks to herself,*] Could this be real? Can this really be happening? [*Her mind wanders before bed. She falls asleep and dreams.*]

DREAM SEQUENCE

[*We don't hear spoken words. Just gestures. Instrumental love song starts playing.*

LAURIE *is sitting at a café near a bridge over water. The weather is clear with boats on the water. The neighborhood is a wealthy one.* STEFAN *is sitting across from her at a table set with two glasses of wine. He points to the bridge, then turns and looks at her. He then grabs her hand and tenderly kisses it. She looks at him lovingly.*]

END SCENE

SCENE 6

NEXT MORNING AFTER TALKING TO STEFAN, LAURIE IS IN HER BED, IN A DREAM STATE—IT'S SUNDAY MORNING ABOUT 8:00AM HER TIME. SHE HEARS HER PHONE BEEPING, LETTING HER KNOW SHE JUST RECEIVED A TEXT AND AN EMAIL.

[*During the next two months, there are many texts, emails, and calls both from* STEFAN *and* LAURIE. *They become more and more romantic.* STEFAN *really gets to* LAURIE's *heart. She feels she loves him. She knows more and more about him and his life, and his son. They have exchanged pictures of their families.*

Some photos to STEFAN *from* LAURIE *were of her in her nighty, and he responded back with pictures of him making kissing faces, shirt off. She has fallen hard for him at this point.*

Also during this time, LAURIE *has lost about twenty pounds and really feels great about herself. She has been walking outside and eating healthy. She purchased a few items of clothes and shoes; she has even taken salsa dance classes with her mom at the senior center.*]

LAURIE's MOM *and daughters really notice a major change in* LAURIE. *How she sounds, how she carries herself. She has certainly gained confidence in the last few months. They are not sure why as she has not told them anything about* STEFAN *yet. She wants to wait for the perfect time when they are all together face-to-face.*]

END SCENE

SCENE 7

FAMILY STYLE RESTAURANT IN TOWN— AROUND 5:00 P.M.

[LAURIE, MOM, SARA, AND CARA (SARA *is home from college for Thanksgiving break*) *all go out to eat.* LAURIE *breaks the news that she met someone online. They all get excited. They start asking many questions. She responds, but tells them not to get excited, but in her heart she is. They ask to see a photo. She takes out her phone and shows them. They are all surprised in their own way.*]

MOM: Wow he's handsome!

Good for you honey lamb! I can see you're gonna get some action [*wink, wink*] [*gives* LAURIE *the elbow*]

LAURIE: [*blushing*]

Mom, stop!

I don't want to talk about him like that.

MOM: Oh honey, we are all women here! And that's a real part of dating and falling in love.

You've gotta be attracted to the guy and that's okay to talk about.

LAURIE: Thanks Mom! I know but [*leans in and looks at both daughters, holding one of their hands in each of hers*]

SCENE 7

I worry about you girls and how you both feel about this.

CARA: Mom! I am so happy for you!

I haven't seen you this happy in a long time.

SARA: Yeah! Cara's right Mom!

You look so happy and that makes us happy!

We understand. Dad moved on, he found somebody new and you should too!

CARA: [*with excitement*] So when do we get to meet him?

LAURIE: [*while looking at a pic of* STEFAN *on her phone and smiling*]

Very soon!

He booked his plane ticket, but, there's one little thing.

[*sheepishly*] He has a son, and he's only 10 years old.

How do you guys feel about that?

[*Both girls speak at the same time. Laurie's* MOM *smiles, remains silent, but her eyes widen with excitement.*]

SARA: That's great Mom!

CARA: Yeah! We always wanted a little brother.

LAURIE: Girls, I think we are getting a little ahead of ourselves. I want us all to meet each other first, and get to know each other better.

CARA: Mom, let's FaceTime him now!

LAURIE: No, I wanted to, many times, but he said he doesn't have that function on his phone.

CARA: [*surprised look on her face*]

MOM: Think positive Laurie!

Things will work out just fine!

You'll see.

[*A waitress comes to the table. We hear background noise.*
　They ask her what he does for a living. LAURIE tells them everything STEFAN has told her about him.]

END SCENE

SCENE 8

NEXT DAY—LAURIE'S KITCHEN—
MID-MORNING—CLOUDY DAY

[LAURIE *gets a text message from* STEFAN *saying he wants to come see her for Christmas since he has time off. She gets excited and texts him back. She begins to imagine what she will do while he's here with his son. Thoughts start going through her head.* STEFAN *says he will text her tomorrow with the flight details.*]

LATER THAT EVENING—LAURIE'S BEDROOM. SHE IS IN
BED—DARK OUTSIDE—SNOWING A LITTLE.

[*Lying in bed watching a movie,* LAURIE *gets a phone call. It's* STEFAN. LAURIE *is holding her cellphone.* STEFAN'*s picture is showing.*]

LAURIE: [*with surprise in her voice*]

Hi honey!? This is a surprise!

I thought you were going to text me.

How are you?

STEFAN: [*with somber tone*]

Not so good my love.

LAURIE: [*sounding concerned*]

Why? What's wrong?

27

FRIED CATFISH

STEFAN: I got mugged!

LAURIE: WHAT? WHEN?

STEFAN: Earlier today, I didn't want to worry you. I'm OKAY!

LAURIE: Awww! You poor thing! Did they hurt you?

STEFAN: Yes, I had to go to the hospital and they stole my passport and wallet with credit cards.

LAURIE: WHAT?! OH MY! What are you going to do?

STEFAN: I have to handle a lot of paperwork and it's going to cost me money. Money I don't have, they froze all my accounts until I get everything in order. So, I can't come visit you just yet, I'm sorry baby!

LAURIE: [with disappointment in her voice]

I understand Stefan, I am sad. Is there anything I can do?

STEFAN: Oh baby! You don't know how much that means to hear you say that!

LAURIE: Of course, Stefan! I love you!

STEFAN: I love you too sweetheart!... .

I need $4,700.

LAURIE: Oh! That much, why?

STEFAN: Honey, remember I have a son to support. I need to pay my bills or we will be homeless. I promise! I promise to you my dear Laurie, you will get this money back and more! I have money. I just cannot access it now. You are an angel!

LAURIE: [*without hesitation and thinking of his son*]

Okay, Stefan. Yes! I will send you the money. How will you get it?

STEFAN: I will email you an account number, go to the MTS (money transfer store) and I will get it.

LAURIE: Okay, I will send it to you first thing tomorrow. Don't worry, I am here for you.

STEFAN: You are my *love!* My soul mate, my heavenly angel! I will call you tomorrow baby! Good night… [*blows kisses*]

LAURIE: Good night. [*blows kisses*]

CALL ENDS

[*After such a traumatizing phone call* LAURIE *tries to fall asleep but has a sleepless night. Many questions go through her mind at once. She just promised a lot of money to a man she has never met in person. Has not even Skyped with, just pictures and his voice.* **How well does she really know him?** *Her bank account only contains about $15,000 in savings. She is currently laid off, between jobs.* LAURIE *decides that she is not going to tell anyone what she is about to do. After a few hours go by,* LAURIE *convinces herself she is doing the right thing. This is real! And she finally falls asleep.*]

END SCENE

SCENE 9

NEXT MORNING—SUNNY—CHILLY OUT—
FINDING A "MONEY TRANSFER STORE" IN TOWN.

[*About 7:30 a.m.—LAURIE goes to the kitchen makes herself some coffee and a bagel for breakfast. Both daughters are still sleeping. SARA is home from college for now, but CARA will be getting up soon to head to school. While sipping some coffee, LAURIE looks at her cellphone. STEFAN has sent her an email with his full name "Stefani Bufoni," and an address in Italy. He thanks her briefly in the email and says he will call her once he sees the money come in. She starts to Google the closest money transfer store in her town. It's not far; they open at 8:00 a.m. She jumps in the shower quickly, dresses, hair in ponytail. She writes a quick note and leaves it in the kitchen in case her daughters get up and find her car gone. LAURIE gets in her car and drives off. She is about 10 minutes away.*

LAURIE parks her car in the parking lot. There are already a few cars there. She has never been here before. She arrives at 8:10 a.m. She enters the money transfer store. Not being familiar with this, she looks around the room and sees a few counters. The rugs are dirty; there are a few chairs, one person is sitting waiting on someone. She sees a window available, no one else standing in line, no number to be called; she decides to approach before being called. This is a typical counter with a glass partition and a small opening to slide items through.]

LAURIE: [*feeling tired*]

> Hi, this is my first time here. I need to send money to this account. [*slides piece of paper under the glass opening in the window*]

[*Behind the counter is standing a six-foot-tall, strong-looking, African-American woman. She has short hair, a wide mouth, and a loud voice when she speaks. Her name tag reads J.J.*]

J.J.: [*looking down at LAURIE, then up and down, with a suspicious look on her face takes the paper which LAURIE slid through and reads it.*]

> So, you want to send money to a "Stefan Bufoni via Bernardino Rota 44 ROMA ITALY?"

> [*emphatically*]

> Fill this out, and don't forget to read the fine print!

> [*slides the paper back along with a few forms for LAURIE to fill out*]

[*LAURIE takes the papers, looks immediately at the fine print and in large bold letters it reads "NOT RESPONSIBLE FOR FRAUDULENT TRANSACTIONS."*
LAURIE is already having mixed feelings about sending the money, so when she reads that line, it makes her upset. Feeling like she's already being looked down on by a counter worker, she gets testy.]

LAURIE: [*looks up at J.J. with a funny look and sharp tone*] FRAUD?!

SCENE 9

Well of course I can read—Thank you!

[*grabs paperwork, walks to a small counter in the back.*]

[*The counter is dirty with pens and crumpled papers strewn around it untidily. LAURIE is afraid to touch anything; she grabs a Kleenex from her purse and grabs a pen with the Kleenex covering it and begins to fill out the paperwork.*
  Ten minutes go by and she comes back to the window.
  LAURIE slides J.J. the filled out paperwork and does not speak.
  J.J. takes the pages and starts reviewing them with one hand. She proceeds to pick her teeth with a fingernail from her other hand.]

LAURIE: [*with look of disgust, under her breath*]

OH GOD!

J.J.: [*in harsh tone*]

I.D.?

[*With hesitation as she just saw this woman picking her teeth and she is extending the same hand, LAURIE reluctantly hands over her driver's license.*]

LAURIE: Umm, doesn't look like you have hand sanitizer here, do you want some? [*looking through her purse*] I may have some here.

J.J.: [*not paying attention to what LAURIE just said*]

[*with attitude*]

Well, this picture doesn't really look like you. Are you sure this is you?

LAURIE: [*sarcastically*]

Ahh! Yes, I think I know who I am.

J.J.: [*with attitude*]

I'm glad someone does.

LAURIE: [*happy tone*]

Well, I just lost about 20 pounds, maybe that's the reason?

J.J.: [*sarcastically*]

Look, I didn't ask for your medical history.

LAURIE: [*getting a bit irritated*]

Look, you seem to be having a bad morning. I have someone waiting on this money; can we please move this along?

J.J.: [*surprised look*]

What's the rush?

[*At that moment, LAURIE's phone beeps. It's a text message from STEFAN.*]

SCENE 9

Text from STEFAN to LAURIE: Good morning my love! I am at my bank.

They are saying I do not have any funds in my account.

Did you send the funds yet?

LAURIE: [*feeling a little flustered*]

See, my boyfriend is texting me, he needs the money now.

J.J.: [*with attitude*]

Boyfriend? What man asks a woman for $4,700?

LAURIE: [*angry tone*]

As if this was any of your business!

We are in love! Now help me transfer this money!

Now!

J.J.: [*a lighter tone, almost laughter in her voice*]

I beg your pardon—Your Highness.

I can see you're…

[*makes air quotes*]

"in love"

Give me a few minutes… and your boyfriend will have his money. And I do mean "BOY."

[LAURIE *doesn't say a word, just looks annoyed.*
J.J. steps sideways to another computer and starts typing ferociously with her long nails. She then prints out a page.
Walking back to the glass window she slides the paper through the slot back to LAURIE.]

J.J.: Okay, here ya go!

Your $4,700 has been sent.

I hope you know what you're doing!

LAURIE: [*shocked look on her face*]

[*emphatically*]

Yes!

YES!... I do!

[LAURIE *turns from the window counter, takes her papers, then leaves the store quickly in a huff.*]

END SCENE

[*A week and a half has gone by.* LAURIE *and* STEFAN *have been communicating the same way by phone and texting. Everything seemed normal.* LAURIE *asks* STEFAN *how things are going.* STEFAN *replies he has his passport, I.D., and credit cards back. He says things are much better.* LAURIE *becomes more hopeful. She hopes to see* STEFAN *in the coming weeks*

*since everything seems back to normal and vaca-
tion time for him is coming up and tells LAURIE
he thinks he may be able to come visit her for
Christmas.*]

SCENE 10

MORE BAD LUCK FOLLOWS STEFAN

ABOUT 11:00 A.M., IT'S A SUNNY, GORGEOUS, CHILLY DAY. LAURIE AND HER DAUGHTERS SARA AND CARA HAVE WALKED A FEW BLOCKS FROM THEIR HOME. THERE IS A FROZEN POND THEY HAVE SKATED ON SINCE THEY WERE KIDS. LAURIE SITS DOWN ON A BENCH IN FRONT OF THE FROZEN POND. SHE IS ALL BUNDLED UP— HAT, GLOVES, CUP OF HOT COFFEE.

[*Both daughters have put their skates on and see their friends. They tell their mom they will be back; they just want to catch up with their friends.*]

LAURIE: Go, go! Go skate with your friends girls; I am fine just sitting here. It's a beautiful day.

[*While sitting on bench,* LAURIE's *phone beeps. It's a text message from* STEFAN.]

Text from STEFAN to LAURIE: Hey baby, you aren't gonna believe this!

Text from LAURIE to STEFAN: [*with smile on her face while texting*]

What?

Text from STEFAN to LAURIE: I had some bad luck again; I am in the hospital with my son.

Text from LAURIE to STEFAN: [LAURIE's *face gets*

SCENE 10

sad as she types]

What? Why?

Text from STEFAN to LAURIE: We were in a car acci-
dent. My son needs surgery.

I can't come visit.

[LAURIE *puts her hand to her mouth and starts
tearing up. From the pond, daughter CARA sees this
and skates over to LAURIE where she is sitting on
the bench.*]

CARA: [*concerned look and voice*]

Mom, what's wrong?

LAURIE: [*wiping her eyes with her glove*]

Oh, nothing honey, I was just reading something sad.

[LAURIE *tells herself that she didn't want anyone
to know that has sent any money to STEFAN. She
didn't want anyone to think badly of him and ques-
tion her motives. She is in love with him—and
doesn't want to involve anyone in their discus-
sions or problems. She certainly doesn't want her
girls to worry.*
   CARA *sits down near LAURIE on the bench and
wraps one of her arms around her and gives her a
side hug. She tilts her head toward her mom's head.*
   LAURIE's *tears start to freeze up on her face
and her nose starts to sniffle.*]

CARA: Oh, okay Mom.

But, if there is something you can always tell me!

LAURIE: [*putting her head on* CARA*'s shoulder*]

I know honey, and I appreciate that!

It's nothing, just some people have bad luck in life, I guess.

Go honey, keep skating a little longer.

[CARA *gets up, faces her mom.*]

CARA: Mom, my generation doesn't believe in bad luck. We need to take responsibility for what part we play in our choices.

LAURIE: How did you get to be so grown up?

CARA: By watching Dr. Phil.

[CARA *pushes off on her skates, turns and faces her mom. She makes a heart out of her two hands and mouths, "I love you!" then turns and skates away.*
LAURIE *continues to read the text from* STEFAN *and replies back.*]

Text from LAURIE to STEFAN: Can I call you?

Text from STEFAN to LAURIE: No baby, I can't talk on the phone right now. I need to talk to the doctor to ask him how I'm gonna pay the bill. I can call you later?

Text from LAURIE to STEFAN: Pay the bill? Don't you have medical insurance?

Text from STEFAN to LAURIE: No baby, it's not like that here. We have to pay out of pocket.

Text from LAURIE to STEFAN: Oh my Stefan, what are you going to do?

Text from STEFAN to LAURIE: I don't know my love… I'm scared.

Text from LAURIE to STEFAN: How much is going to cost?

Text from STEFAN to LAURIE: $6,000!

Text from LAURIE to STEFAN: Why so much?

Text from STEFAN to LAURIE: The guy who hit us doesn't have insurance.

[LAURIE *is so shocked and angry that this happened to* STEFAN *again. She is thinking about his son and visualizing a little ten-year-old boy lying in a hospital bed with tubes. She thinks of her own daughters. Her emotions get the best of her.*]

Text from LAURIE to STEFAN: Stefan, do you need me to send you any money?

Text from STEFAN to LAURIE: Oh, my dearest love, you don't know how much that means to me that you would offer! I am embarrassed. I don't want you to think I am not a man. I am just having bad luck in my life now. I need you Laurie! You are my savior! My Guardian Angel!

Text from LAURIE to STEFAN: Stefan, I love you! I know things are going to get better! It's just money and I trust you.

Text from STEFAN to LAURIE: I promise to Almighty God that you will get your money back! And more!

Text from LAURIE to STEFAN: I know, I believe in you.

Text from STEFAN to LAURIE: Ok Baby! Send me the money and I will tell you when I get it.

Text from LAURIE to STEFAN: Ok. I will send it by tomorrow.

Text from STEFAN to LAURIE: I love you Baby! I'll talk to you tomorrow.

[sends love emojis]

Text from LAURIE to STEFAN: Ok. [*sends love emojis*]

END SCENE

SCENE 11

MORE MONEY TO TAKE OUT FOR STEFAN

LAURIE HAS HAD ANOTHER SLEEPLESS NIGHT. IT'S 5:00 A.M., SHE IS IN HER BED. SHE PICKS UP HER CELLPHONE FROM HER NIGHTSTAND, LIES SIDEWAYS IN HER BED, AND STARTS SCROLLING THROUGH STEFAN'S PICTURES. SHE STILL HAS A WARM FUZZY FEELING INSIDE FOR HIM EVEN THOUGH SHE HAS NOT MET HIM YET OR SEEN HIM ON SKYPE OR FACETIME.

LAURIE: [*softly, to herself*]

> This is real. I know it's real, I can feel it. I can trust this man, there is nothing he has done or said to me so far that would make me doubt him.

[*She gives herself a hug. She speaks softly out loud and begins to pray.*]

LAURIE: God, it's me Laurie, I know we haven't spoken in a while, I have not asked for much as I thought you forgot about me. I was so happy before when I was married, and had Sara, then Cara, my miracle girls; I thought I was lucky. Then my marriage ended, and I thought that was it for me, that I wasn't allowed any more happiness. God… can you please give me one more chance! One more chance for happiness! Let Stefan be everything he says he is! Let us live a loving and happy life! Please God!

[LAURIE *gets up out of bed about 6:00 a.m., still too early to go to the bank to see what money she*

43

has left to send to STEFAN. *She makes coffee, goes to the couch, watches the news; it's a waiting game until 9:00 a.m.*

Partly-cloudy day, LAURIE *is wearing a thick sweater, scarf, gloves. She gets in her car and begins driving to the town. She begins to hear a song that speaks to her. Her face begins to turn sad/somber as she listens to the song. Not a long ride. She arrives at the bank parking lot and parks.*

LAURIE *exits her car and enters the bank—it's a little after 9:00 a.m. There are only a few customers inside.*

There is one person in front of her.]

BANK TELLER: [*pleasant tone*]

Next in line please.

[LAURIE *approaches the counter and places her handbag on the counter shelf. She is familiar with the teller as she uses this bank.*]

BANK TELLER: [*high-pitched, happy tone.*]

WELL HI THERE LAURIE!

HOW ARE YOU TODAY? HOW'S EVERYONE?

LAURIE: [*speaking softly*]

Good morning, Beverly, well not so good.

I need to make a large withdrawal.

BANK TELLER: [*sounding surprised*]

OH MY! I AM SORRY TO HEAR THAT!

IS YOUR MOM OK? THE GIRLS?

NOTHING BAD I HOPE!

LAURIE: [*sounding embarrassed*]

Oh no, they're fine! I am helping a friend. She needs the money.

[*whispering with her lips turning sideways*]

She has really bad credit, and can't afford the interest. Just trying to help out a friend. Y'know.

BANK TELLER: [*Making a sad face*]

WELL! LAURIE [*Shaking her head*]

YOU ARE SUCH A SWEET PERSON! HMM, HMMM, HMM.

I WISH THERE WERE MORE PEOPLE LIKE YOU IN THIS WORLD!

NOW HOW MUCH ARE WE WITHDRAWING TODAY?

LAURIE: [*speaking softly*]

$6,000.

BANK TELLER: [*High-pitched gasp*]

WHOA!

[*The few people in the bank turn and look at them.*]

LAURIE: [*looking more embarrassed*]

I KNOW, I KNOW.

IT'S A LOT!

BANK TELLER: [*as she is typing, she looks at the screen, speaks with hushed tone*]

Yes, that will leave you with less than $5,000 in your account since you paid some bills.

Are you sure you want to do this Laurie?

LAURIE: [*sighs, takes a few seconds, softly*]

Yes.

[*then says it louder as if she is convincing herself*]

YES! YES! I DO!

SHE NEEDS MY HELP!

BANK TELLER: OKAY then, give me few minutes here,

I will give you a cashier's check.

[LAURIE *pulls out her cellphone from her purse and looks at it; there is no text from* STEFAN. *She waits for the* TELLER, *the* TELLER *comes back and* LAURIE *puts her cellphone back in her purse.*]

BANK TELLER: [*in a sweet tone while handing* LAURIE *the check*]

OKAY LAURIE HONEY, HERE YOU GO!

[*shaking her head*] You are such a great person Laurie!

I'm glad this is for a friend and not a catfish!

LAURIE: [*sounding shocked*]

WHAT?!

A CATFISH?

BANK TELLER: [*starts to whisper*]

Oh yeah, you never heard of that?

LAURIE: [*still in doubt*]

No!

You mean an actual fish you eat?

BANK TELLER: [*starts to giggle a bit*]

No, honey, a person from another country, who gets ya [*makes gesture of being grabbed with her hands*] to fall in love with them, only by phone and pictures. You never meet them in person, [*voice lowers*] but, they steal your heart, and take all your money!

LAURIE: [*mouth hanging wide open, then with disbelief speaks*]

COME ON NOW, BEVERLY!

THAT'S RIDICULOUS!

WHO WOULD BE STUPID ENOUGH TO FALL FOR THAT?

BANK TELLER: [*shaking her head, softly*]

Yeah, I know honey, sounds crazy, but, it happens!

LAURIE: Okay thank you.

BANK TELLER: [*sweetly says*]

YOU'RE WELCOME LAURIE!

NOW YOU SAY HI TO MOM AND THE GIRLS!

LAURIE: I WILL!

[LAURIE *walks toward the exit to the bank and stops before she pushes the door to leave. She looks at the* BANK TELLER *for a few seconds as if she is thinking about what she just said. It struck a chord inside* LAURIE. *But again, she ignores it, she doesn't want to believe. She pushes the door out and is now outside the bank.*]

LAURIE: [*talking very softly to herself outside as she's walking*]

Stefan can't be a catfish! No, I know he's real! I know he loves me! I'm not stupid!

SECTION 11

END SCENE

[LAURIE *goes directly to the money transfer store and this time has no issues. It is a quick transaction with someone there who she has not encountered before. She is able to feel better, that she is helping* STEFAN *and his son.*

Later that day, LAURIE *gets a phone call from* STEFAN. *He is so happy and keeps praising her over and over stating what an angel she is, how she saved is son, and now there is nothing to prevent him from coming to see her for Christmas.*

LAURIE *is able to sleep peacefully that night thinking it's all worth it!*]

SCENE 12

THIRD TIME IS THE CHARM—
THE LAST EXCUSE FROM STEFAN

A WEEK BEFORE CHRISTMAS. LAURIE'S HOUSE,
SHE HAS BEEN PREPARING WITH HER MOM AND DAUGH-
TERS FOR STEFAN AND HIS SON TO VISIT. THEY HAVE
DECORATED OUTSIDE WITH LIGHTS. INSIDE THEY HAVE
A BEAUTIFUL TREE, NICELY DECORATED AND HAVE
EVEN DISCUSSED THE MEALS THEY WILL PREPARE
FOR THE TIME THEY ARE HERE.

[*Laurie's* MOM *is in the kitchen making up a batch of eggnog with rum. She and* LAURIE *each have a glass and are feeling very happy. It's about 3:00 p.m.* LAURIE's *phone rings. She picks up and sees it's* STEFAN.]

LAURIE: [*feeling a little buzzed after drinking eggnog*]

Hiii, sweetheart, how are you?

[*Laurie's* MOM *is also feeling a bit happy at this point; she yells from across the room.*]

MOM: Hii, Stefan! It's your mother-in-law to be!

STEFAN: [*with French/African accent*]

Ooh, baby! Is that your mom?! Tell her I said hello.

LAURIE: Mom, Stefan says hello.

MOM: Oh nice, I'll go in the other room so you can have your privacy.

[*Laurie's* MOM *leaves the room.*]

LAURIE: Thanks Mom!

So my love, are you excited?

Only six more days before you get on that plane to see me!

STEFAN: Oh my love, you know I can't wait to see you, to hold you, to kiss you… I have something to tell you.

LAURIE: What?

STEFAN: My mom, she passed away.

LAURIE: [*completely taken off guard*]

What? Oh my God!

[LAURIE *barely sits on the chair, and almost falls down on the floor—she starts to cry*]

STEFAN: No, no darling Laurie, don't cry, please, it's okay…. She was not well, she was sick for a long time.

LAURIE: But, she's your mom, aren't you sad?

STEFAN: Of course I am sad, but, I have you in my life baby, and that makes me happy. I didn't want to call you to make you cry. I am calling to tell you I am still coming to see you. But, I have a problem. I need to pay for my mom's funeral and I used all my money to buy our flight tickets to see you.

LAURIE: Oh, Stefan. What can I do? I feel so bad!

STEFAN: Baby, I would never ask you for more, you have given me so much already. I will figure out something.

LAURIE: Stefan, I am in this too deep now. I love you! I really, really love you and I know things will work out.

How much do you need?

STEFAN: Oh my angel, you are too good to me!

Can you send me $5,000?

LAURIE: I will see what I can do.

STEFAN: I need it tomorrow.

As I promised before, I will pay you back everything and much more when I see you—in six days.

LAURIE: I know you will Stefan, I know you will, I trust you!

[LAURIE *hangs up with* STEFAN. *She does not say a word to her mom. She decides to have another eggnog, this time with more rum. She feels even more buzzed now.*

SECTION 12

She stumbles into her bedroom, looks through her jewelry box on top of her bureau. She finds her wedding and engagement rings and holds them up. She decides this is what she needs to do to get the money for STEFAN. She can't afford to use more of her own savings right now. She takes the rings and puts them in a pouch and places them in her purse. Tomorrow she will go to a pawn shop and sell them.]

END SCENE

SCENE 13

PAWN SHOP SCENE

NEXT DAY—PARTLY-CLOUDY—LAURIE WAKES UP AROUND 8:30AM A BIT GROGGY, SHE LOOKS AT THE CLOCK AND JUMPS RIGHT UP AT THE TIME. SHE WANTS TO BE AT THE PAWN SHOP AS SOON AS THEY OPEN.

[LAURIE *doesn't even shower; she grabs her purse and jumps in her car. She knows where this place is, though she has never been inside. LAURIE pulls in the parking lot. LAURIE thought about it a lot and pulls out a small pouch from her purse. She sees this as an opportunity to put the past behind her and sell those rings which ended in divorce.*

The pawn shop is called Guaranteed Cash and the sign states: "no monkey business."

LAURIE walks into the pawn shop. It's her first time there. She looks around and notices how unkept the shop is, and cluttered. It has a sour odor.]

LAURIE: [*with apprehension in her voice*]

Ahh, hello?

[PAWN SHOP OWNER *a thin, medium-height man, scruffy looking, unshaven, wearing T-shirt, dirty jeans. Looks unseemly.*]

PAWN SHOP OWNER: [*Blank look on his face*]

Hi.

LAURIE: I want to talk to someone about selling my ring.

PAWN SHOP OWNER: You can talk to me and Jimmy here.

[*laughs—turns his head to the capuchin monkey sitting on the counter*]

LAURIE: [*screams*]

AHHGH!

[*puts her hand on her chest*]

[*loudly*] IS THAT ANIMAL LEGAL?!

Should you have a wild animal loose in a store?

PAWN SHOP OWNER: I'm loose!

Ain't nobody stopped me yet! [*winks*]

Jimmy here, he ain't no animal, he's a good guy.

LAURIE: Umm, do you have a manager here? An owner?

PAWN SHOP OWNER: That would be me on both counts.

LAURIE: [*looking skeptical*]

Okay.

[*takes rings from her purse and holds it up*]

I need to sell these rings and I see that you pay cash.

PAWN SHOP OWNER: [*putting a jeweler's eyeglass in one eye, he takes the diamond ring from her hand and inspects it*]

[*makes a sound*]

Uh-huh.

[*He hands the ring to the monkey, who takes it and walks to the other end of the counter.*]

LAURIE: [*sounding upset*]

Hey, where is he going with that!?

[MONKEY *places both rings on a scale.*]

PAWN SHOP OWNER: Don't worry lady; he knows what he's doing.

[*looking at scale*]

Well Jimmy, what da ya think?

JIMMY: [*Holds up five fingers*]

PAWN SHOP OWNER: Ok, we'll give you $5,000 for them.

LAURIE: [*loudly with surprise*]

$5,000?

You're letting a monkey make that decision?

PAWN SHOP OWNER: [*looking at the monkey as he*

speaks and rubbing his head]

Jimmy's been doing this for a long time; he's the best in the business!

[hands the monkey a tiny banana]

Thanks Jimmy! Go on your break now!

[JIMMY *takes the banana and goes into the back room and turns on the TV.*]

PAWN SHOP OWNER: I think you just offended Jimmy.

LAURIE: *[with sarcasm]*

Oh well, I certainly don't want to offend your monkey!

[high-pitched tone]

Is that all you can give me?!

PAWN SHOP OWNER: Afraid so, that's the best rate you're gonna get around here.

LAURIE: *[tapping her fingernails on the counter, with hesitation]*

I'll take it.

PAWN SHOP OWNER: *[walks to the back office behind him and grabs his checkbook. He opens it, takes a look and scratches his head.]*

Oh boy! I'm a little short today, but, if you

come back tomorrow I should have it.

LAURIE: [*sounding nervous*] I can't! I need it today!

PAWN SHOP OWNER: [*looking surprised at her impatience*]

Oh, okay, I can give you $2,500 cash today and the other half tomorrow.

[LAURIE *starts pacing, puts hand on her head.*]

PAWN SHOP OWNER: You sound like me when I need a fix.

LAURIE: [*with weird look on her face*]

I'M NOT A JUNKIE! This is a matter of life or death!

PAWN SHOP OWNER: [*sounding surprised*] Okay lady, nobody's judging you here...

LAURIE: [*sounding more calm*] Well, I certainly hope not!

PAWN SHOP OWNER: [*sounding sincere*]

Look, I will have the other half tomorrow.

[*turning his head to the office behind him— he looks at the monkey*] You can take Jimmy with you as collateral and bring him back tomorrow.

SCENE 13

LAURIE: [*shakes her head*]

You want me to take your monkey home with me?

PAWN SHOP OWNER: Jimmy doesn't know he's a monkey—he's like a hairy little boy.

LAURIE: [*sounding out the word*]

Uh! He's a M o n k e y!

PAWN SHOP OWNER: [*with head slightly tilted*]

Listen, Jimmy is very important to me and my business. I wouldn't let him go home with you if I wasn't going to make good on the money. Besides, you'd be helping me out. I need to go out of town and Jimmy ain't fond of who I need to visit.

[*pointing at a poster of a capuchin monkey on the wall in a high budget movie*]

Jimmy is actually a well-trained movie star; he has a cult-like following. Look him up sometime, you will be surprised. Highly trained and sadly works for bananas.

LAURIE: [*with hesitation*]

I can't believe I am saying this but, okay.

[*emphatically*]

I'm coming back first thing tomorrow when you open—to get the rest of my money and drop off

Jimmy!

PAWN SHOP OWNER: No problem.

[LAURIE *and* PAWN SHOP OWNER *exchange info, he gives her $2,500 in cash and a small satchel which has* JIMMY's *clothes, a hat, stuffed animal, and some bananas. The owner puts on* JIMMY's *hat and little coat and he grabs his stuffed animal.* JIMMY *jumps in the satchel.* LAURIE *takes the satchel with* JIMMY's *head popping out and she walks out of the pawn shop.*]

END SCENE

SCENE 14

LAST VISIT TO MONEY TRANSFER STORE—
SAME DAY, SHORTLY AFTER THE PAWN SHOP

[LAURIE *only has half of what* STEFAN *asked for:*
$2,500 in cash. She decides to at least get this
money to him today and tell him the other half will
have to be tomorrow. She thinks to herself, how is
this going to work? She is worried that she may
have to deal with J.J. again or maybe someone may
recognize her in this town. Since the bank teller
knows she withdrew so much, word may get back to
her mom and she doesn't want to deal with that.

LAURIE goes to her car for a minute. She opens
her trunk and places JIMMY *(in the satchel) in the*
open trunk while she is looking for something. His
head is peeking through, watching her. LAURIE *finds*
her large brimmed hat and large dark sunglasses in
a bag. Just by chance, she finds another bag with
her daughter's Halloween wig that was left there
a few years back. It's long and black. LAURIE
thinks this is a perfect disguise for her to go one
last time to the money transfer store. She goes
in her car with JIMMY *and puts on the wig, hat,*
dark glasses, and red lipstick. She looks in the
mirror and nods at herself, then looks at JIMMY.
He screeches and she screams herself. She wasn't
prepared for that.

The money transfer store is a few blocks away.
She drives there and parks in the small parking
lot. Now in disguise, LAURIE *goes into the build-*
ing. No other customers are there at the moment.
She fills out the paperwork needed to send the
money. She approaches the counter. The shade is
down, it suddenly rolls up.

There is J.J. standing tall and ready to greet
LAURIE.]

LAURIE: [*with fake French accent, tries to speak
French*]

Qui, bonjour…

I would like to send this to this address.
[*she slides the $2,500 cash, with paperwork
to send to STEFAN—the same address as before*]

J.J.: [*looks at LAURIE with suspicious eyes, up
and down and makes a snarly face*]

I.D. please.

LAURIE: [*with fake French accent*]

I.D.? What for? I never had to show this
before.

What is the meaning of this?

[*in French*]

I don't understand.

[LAURIE's *mind is all over the place; she forgot
she needed to provide an I.D. to send the money
again. So now in disguise she looks nothing like
her picture.*]

J.J.: Well understand this… I need something that
shows a picture of you.

SCENE 14

LAURIE: [*with surprise*]

    Sacré bleu!

[LAURIE *puts her large bag on the counter and starts rummaging through it to see if she can locate something. She does not know what to do next.*]

J.J.: [*standing there, arms folded watching her*]

    We don't have all day here. Come on…

LAURIE: [*fake French accent*]

    You Americans, you are always in a rush… we French, we take our time… we savor the moment…

[*Trying to figure out what to do next, she turns her head toward the door.* JIMMY *pops out of her bag and hops on the counter.*]

J.J.: Well, what the… ?

[JIMMY *pulls on* LAURIE'*s wig and it starts to come halfway down her shoulder; her dark glasses get caught on the wig and also get pulled sideways.*]

LAURIE: [*does not realize she has been exposed, trying to fix her glasses, speaks with fake French accent*]

    Well, it seems that I have forgotten my I.D.

[JIMMY *then pulls off* LAURIE'*s wig and hat and they fall to the floor.*]

J.J.: I knew that was you!

You got issues!

LAURIE: Okay, okay… yes, it's me…

J.J.: [*shaking her head*]

Hmmm, hmmm.

[JIMMY *is looking at* LAURIE.]

LAURIE: [*Turns to JIMMY*]

TRAITOR!

Get back in the bag!

I'll deal with you later!

[JIMMY *gets back in the bag, his head still poking out.*]

LAURIE: [*turns back to* J.J. *behind the window*]

[*angrily*] What do you want from me?!

I didn't want to deal with you again!

I don't need your attitude today!

All I want to do is send some money to my boyfriend, and now I'm angry!

J.J.: Oh, so you're angry are you?!

SCENE 14

LAURIE: [*emphatically*]

YES!

J.J.: Well, it's about time!

LAURIE: WHAT?

What do you mean?

Why should I be angry?

[J.J. *leaves the counter, goes to the front door and turns the sign from "OPEN" to "CLOSED" and locks the door. She goes back to office door and motions for* LAURIE *to come inside.*]

J.J.: Follow me.

[LAURIE *walks into the back office. She looks around. It's a bit larger than the front. J.J. sits at her chair behind a desk, then points to the chairs in front of the desk and gestures to* LAURIE *to take a seat.* LAURIE *sits down on one chair. She places the satchel with* JIMMY *inside on the other chair.* JIMMY *slowly gets out of the bag, looks around, and sits on the chair next to* LAURIE.]

LAURIE: [*sounds scared*]

What?

Am I in trouble?

J.J.: NO!

But, the guy who is scamming you is!

LAURIE: [*with surprise*]

What?

Scamming me? Who's scamming me?

[J.J. *has a large desktop computer with three monitors. She starts typing. JIMMY gets up and walks across the desk and sits next to J.J. She ignores him and focuses on LAURIE.*]

J.J.: What's this jackass's name that you've been talking to?

STEFAN right?

He is a "CATFISH."

LAURIE: [*sounding confused*]

A catfish?

Why do people keep saying that word?

He's not a fish; I still don't understand what that means.

J.J.: He may not be a fish,

but he smells… and he smells bad!

LAURIE: Smells, how do you know what he smells like?

I haven't even met him yet!

J.J.: EXACTLY!

I need to educate you!

He is a scammer, a fraud, he is not real!

LAURIE: He's real; I talked to him on the phone!

J.J.: You may have heard his voice, but, you haven't met him in person—and [*with attitude*]

You are not going to!

LAURIE: Oh, no… you're wrong…

He is flying in next week to spend Christmas with me and my girls.

J.J.: [*with pity in her voice*]

Oh, honey… no. I'm sorry to be the one to tell you this… you have been scammed!

Why were you sending him money today?

You are not the only one who has fallen for this type of scam and you won't be the last.

LAURIE: What is going on here?

[*her voice starts to get higher*]

I came in to send money and you're starting to freak me out!

[J.J. *turns one of the computer monitors toward* LAURIE *and shows her a picture and profile of* STEFAN, *the man that* LAURIE *has been talking to.*]

J.J.: Is this your guy?

LAURIE: [*excited*]

YES!

THAT'S HIM! STEFAN!

How did you get his picture?

J.J.: Well, on this website, his name is David.

LAURIE: What?

[J.J. *starts typing again.*]

J.J.: And on this website, this is Mark.

LAURIE: What are you talking about?

[J.J. *starts typing again.*]

J.J.: Laurie, do you understand what is going on here?

LAURIE: NO! I DON'T!

J.J.: This guy, whoever he is, his pictures have been stolen, taken off his Facebook or Instagram or somewhere. These pictures could be ten to fifteen years old.

And now they are being used by a scammer, a
CATFISH.

He is not real!

The profile is made up—let me show you
something.

[J.J. *starts typing and clicks on a Youtube video of
a Dr. Phil episode. It shows highlights, explains
what scammers say they do for jobs, excuses they
make to their victims of why they need money, and
what lines they use to romantically draw in their
victims.*

*After watching this, LAURIE is in total disbe-
lief. She puts her elbow on the desk and her hand
to her head. Her eyes start to go back and forth
trying to make sense of what she has just been
told. JIMMY has been sitting on J.J.'s side this
entire time, then gets up and sits on the desk
facing LAURIE. He touches her hand and starts to
stroke it, feeling that she is upset.*]

J.J.: [*sounding scared*]

Laurie, are you OKAY?

LAURIE: [*her voice starts shaking*]

So what you are telling me is… I have sent my
entire savings to a scammer?

Is that what you are telling me?!

[*She stands up and starts to pace the office. JIMMY
starts pacing on the desk.*]

J.J.: [*talking to* JIMMY]

And who might you be?

JIMMY: [*he stops pacing and extends his hand to* J.J.]

LAURIE: That's Jimmy.

J.J.: Is he your pet?

LAURIE: No, I am watching him for the day.

J.J.: He's cute.

Can he do anything?

LAURIE: Well, his owner—

J.J.: [*squawks*]

LAURIE: I mean business partner said he was in the movies.

J.J.: Movies?

[*looking at* JIMMY, *smiling*]

Well, then he's got some skills.

We can use him.

LAURIE: [*sounding skeptical*]

OKAY WHATEVER!

SCENE 14

He wasn't much help to me out there.

J.J.: [*looking at* JIMMY *pacing*]

Awww, you poor baby… you're upset!

LAURIE: He's upset?!

How about me?

He said he loved me! That I was the best thing that ever happened to him! That we were going to spend the rest of our lives together! LIES! ALL LIES!

[LAURIE *grabs something from the desk and throws it to the ground and it breaks!* JIMMY *does the same thing.*]

J.J.: I know you're upset… but, you're gonna pay for that!

LAURIE: [*angry*]

Pay? Pay?

With what money?

I'm flat broke!

J.J.: What about the money you were going to send just now?

LAURIE: [*with disdain*]

What?

$2,500, what can I do with that?

AND YOU!

J.J.: Me?

Me what?

LAURIE: You knew all along he was a scammer? Didn't you?

Didn't you? And you didn't tell me?! Why didn't anyone here stop me from sending money to him if you know people are being scammed?

J.J.: You're right! But, it's not the job of a money transfer store to wake you up to reality! Our job is just to send money to wherever it needs to go—no questions asked!

Remember that first time, I said don't forget to read the fine print?

LAURIE: Really! Are you kidding me?!

So anyone can get scammed and there is nothing stopping these criminals! Is that what you are telling me?

That we are on our own in this!

That we work our entire lives to save a little bit of money and in one fell swoop-it's gone?! Is that what you are telling me?!

J.J.: Yup!

No, what I mean is the world has changed.

Crime is happening through cyberspace.

They have taken falling in love and criminalized it. These are professional scumbags; they don't care about you, your feelings, how hard you've worked. They just want your money. They don't care if you're poor, 'cause that's who most of them are. They are inhuman. They want to make people suffer.

[LAURIE *sits back down in the chair across from* J.J. *and puts her head on the desk.* JIMMY *goes over to* LAURIE *and starts stroking her head. When she picks up her head, the monkey gets a tissue from the box on the desk and hands it to her.*]

LAURIE: [LAURIE *starts to cry, putting her head down*]

Well, this guy has taken more than my money. He has taken my self-worth, my belief that people for the most part are good, and he has taken my hope away that someone could ever love me in that way again.

J.J.: Nobody can take anything away from you what you are not willing to give on your own free will. I know that is not what you want to hear but, the truth hurts.

LAURIE: I'm numb!

[*freaked out tone*]

What am I going to do now?

J.J.: Laurie, I am going to make you an offer but, once I do and you refuse, we are done. This is a one-time offer only.

LAURIE: So, are you trying to scam me too?

J.J.: NO!

[J.J. *gets up from the desk; she goes to the door and locks it. LAURIE and JIMMY are both looking at her skeptically. J.J. goes back to her desk and sits down. She opens her top drawer and pulls out a badge and places it on the desk.*]

LAURIE: What's that?

Are you a cop?

F.B.I.?

What?

J.J.: [*leans in across the desk and stares* LAURIE *in the eyes*]

Laurie, I am part of a crime-fighting unit that handles things like this—scammers from beginning to end.

LAURIE: End?

J.J.: [*leans back in chair*]

Yes, END.

This is where the scammer meets the end of

the line and **"WE"** are going after your guy!

LAURIE: WE? We who?

I don't know anything about fighting crime!

Did we meet?

I just got SCAMMED!

J.J.: And that's why no one will see you coming…

LAURIE: I don't like this!

I can't do this!

J.J.: Laurie, let me tell you how I got into this. I knew nothing about how people were. When I was ten I witnessed an older couple in my neighborhood get mugged.

LAURIE: Oh, how awful!

J.J.: But, it wasn't!

You see this couple didn't just let this mugger get away.

They fought back.

They were strong, and I mean physically strong and they held him down until the cops came.

They were my heroes and then became my mentors and my bosses in the ACF.

FRIED CATFISH

LAURIE: ACF?

J.J.: Aged Crime Fighting unit.

Don't let the name fool you. Laurie, you told me you were angry! You told me how much he hurt you, and you are going to let him get away?

LAURIE: Well, you can do it; you know what he looks like.

Why do you need me?

J.J.: Laurie, is that what you want? Someone else to get scammed by this guy? Yes, we can go and get him, but without you, we can't bring him to justice!

LAURIE: No, I don't want anyone else to go what I went through.

I can't believe I felt so many emotions for this person!

What's wrong with me?

J.J.: Nothing is wrong with you Laurie, you are human.

Are you with me Laurie?

Are you angry enough to stop this guy?

LAURIE: YES!

I will do anything to make sure he doesn't do this to someone else!

J.J.: Just leave the details to me… I will call you later. Go home and act normal. Don't contact Stefan until we talk again later.

LAURIE: OKAY.

[LAURIE *gets up;* JIMMY *gets in the satchel.* J.J. *lets them out of the office.*]

END SCENE

SCENE 15

IN CAR DRIVING HOME—LATE AFTERNOON—INSIDE
LAURIE'S CAR. JIMMY IS SITTING IN PASSENGER SEAT
WITH SEATBELT AROUND HIM.

LAURIE: [*to herself and* JIMMY *while driving*]

I can't believe it? This is a dream… can't
be real!

[*We don't see that* LAURIE *has already called her*
MOM *and told her that she is coming over and has
something big to tell her.* LAURIE *arrives at her
mom's house, pulls in the driveway, leaves* JIMMY
in car. It will be a short visit.]

MOM'S HOUSE

[LAURIE *and her* MOM *are at the kitchen table.*
LAURIE *has already told her about the catfish; we
find the conversation already in progress.*]

MOM: [*pacing the kitchen*] I'm so sorry! Why didn't
you tell me muffin that this guy had asked you
for money? I would have told you that he was
a catfish.

LAURIE: [*sitting at the kitchen table, sounding
surprised*]

CATFISH? Really Mom! You too? How do you know
about that?!

MOM: I watch Dr. Phil! I learned so much by watching his show! This has been going on for
years! And I am sure before the internet!

Laurie, real men don't ask women for money and for that matter neither do real women! Anyone who asks for money at any point in the relationship is SCUM! That should always be a red flag!

LAURIE: [*putting hand on her head, head down*]

I feel so dumb! So naive! So vulnerable!

[MOM *walks over to* LAURIE *and puts her arms around her and kisses her head.*]

MOM: Honey, you are a VICTIM! Of course, that SCUMBAG—or SCUMBAGS—have used your own feelings against you! There's nothing worse than thinking you are in love with someone only to have the rug pulled from underneath you! You did nothing wrong except feel something for another human being! I am sooo sorry! You are a wonderful woman and a great mom to your girls!

LAURIE: [*picking up her head*]

My girls! What will they think of me? How am I going to explain how dumb their mom is?

MOM: You need to be honest with yourself and honest with them; that's all!

[LAURIE's *cellphone rings, she notices it says "private." She picks up.*]

LAURIE: Hello?... Hi…

[*She gets up from the kitchen table and walks into*

the living room. We don't hear what the conversation is. MOM looks puzzled, waits for her to end
the call.]

LAURIE: [skepticism in her voice, just listens
to what J.J. is saying and only gives short
responses]

Okay… yeah,

Okay…

I guess so…

Okay

[call ends]

[MOM enters the living room.]

MOM: Who was that Laurie?

The SCUMBAG?

LAURIE: No Mom, it was J.J.

MOM: Who's J.J.?

Another scammer?

[eyes widen] THEEEE SCAMMER?!

LAURIE: No, Mom! J.J. is a woman at the money
transfer place who is helping me track Stefan
down and get my money back!

MOM: Honey, I know you are a smart woman, but,
do you honestly think you're going to see

any money again? How can you trust this J.J. person if you just got scammed? Maybe they're in cahoots?

LAURIE: Mom, I'm not sure, I don't know who to trust anymore!

But it's worth a shot, I've lost everything! I have nothing left to lose! Please Mom, just support me in this, PLEASE!

[MOM *gets closer to* LAURIE, *they face each other.* MOM *grabs* LAURIE's *upper arms.*]

MOM: Of course! I am always there for you! I've always told you that you can do anything you set your mind to! You are obviously determined. I am not going to stop you.

What do you need me to do?

LAURIE: Watch Sara and Cara for me! Don't tell them anything, I don't want them to worry! Just tell them that Mom needs a few days to herself to plan for Stefan's visit. It's perfect timing since they're staying with Dan for the next three days.

MOM: Okay, LAURIE! Be safe, call me and remember I am always here for you! I LOVE YOU!

LAURIE: I LOVE YOU TOO MOM!

[*They hug.*]

END SCENE

SCENE 16

DRIVING TO AIRPORT SCENE

INSIDE LAURIE'S HOUSE—11:00 P.M. LAURIE IS PACING—
SHE KEEPS LOOKING OUT HER DINING ROOM WINDOW,
BRUSHING ASIDE THE CURTAINS.

[*A few minutes later, outside* LAURIE's *house—a black expensive looking sedan pulls up. The* DRIVER *does not get out; the back door opens automatically and she hesitantly gets in the back seat. She has* JIMMY *in the satchel with his head poking out and places him on the seat next to her.*

LAURIE's *view is the back of the* DRIVER's *head.*

The DRIVER *is bald, with a muscular build and deep eastern European accent.*]

LAURIE: [*voice a little shaky*]

Uhh, hello?

Do you know where we are going?

DRIVER: [*with deep voice and heavy accent*]

Yes!

Do you?

[*shaking his head and muttering in his own language under his breath, something that sounds like disgust*]

[DRIVER *pulls away—speeds through her neighborhood.*
LAURIE *gets tossed around the back seat and*

tries to put on her seatbelt. The bag with JIMMY
in it slides to the opposite side of the car.]

LAURIE: [screaming]

ARE YOU *CRAZY????*

[catching her breath]

There's a speed limit ya know!!

[Frantically putting her seatbelt on, it finally
clicks in.
   DRIVER doesn't pay attention to LAURIE, keeps
driving, is now on the highway driving about 90
mph.
   LAURIE is thrust back into the back seat, her
head whips back.]

LAURIE: [mumbling to herself]

I'm going die even before I really die.

[she makes the sign of the cross]

[She puts her hand to her mouth, like she wants to
vomit.
   Turning to her bag, the monkey's face pops out;
he also looks like he wants to vomit.
   Monkey jumps out of the bag and onto the driver's shoulder and vomits on him, then jumps to
passenger seat and sits calmly holding his belly.]

DRIVER: [screams like a girl in a high pitched voice]

Ahhhggg!

FRIED CATFISH

[*Car starts to swerve out of control.*]

LAURIE: [*in a deep voice*] Keep the change...
dickhead!

[DRIVER *gets a hold of the car. They exit off to
what looks like a large open field, fenced off with
barbed wire, and there is long airstrip. It is not
a typical civilian airport. The car approaches a
huge plane—it's a C-30 military plan. The driver
screeches to a stop about 20 feet from the plane.
Back door opens,* LAURIE *jumps out of the back seat
of the car with her bag and slams the door shut,
she then opens the front passenger door for* JIMMY
to get out. DRIVER *is looking at his jacket with
vomit with disgust and looks up at* LAURIE.]

LAURIE: [*screams at the driver*]

SEE, THAT'S WHAT YOU GET!

KEEP THE CHANGE, ASSHOLE!

[LAURIE *leaves the front passenger door open,* JIMMY
*jumps on her back and they start walking away from
the car toward the plane.*]

END SCENE

SCENE 17

BOARDING THE PLANE

PRIVATE TARMAC—11:30 P.M.—A C-130 HERCULES
AIRCRAFT IS STARING LAURIE IN THE FACE—
IT IS ALL IN BLACK WITH THE ACF LOGO.

[LAURIE *approaches the plane slowly. J.J. is there talking to someone who is getting the plane ready. J.J. is dressed in a black, military looking outfit with knee-high black boots.*

LAURIE is dressed normally: pants, top, coat, and high heels. She looks like she is going on a job interview. She approaches J.J. and they simultaneously pass their eyes up and down what the other is wearing.]

LAURIE: [*look of surprise on her face and high pitch*]

And who are you supposed to be?

J.J.: [*turning sideways*]

These are my work clothes for when I'm about to kick some serious butt!

[*does karate chop move and high kick*]

LAURIE: Okay?

[*has funny look on her face*]

[*using harsh, angry voice*]

I almost died on my way here!

J.J.: [*shaking her head*]

If you can't handle the car ride, I don't know how you are going handle this.

[*looking at* JIMMY]

And how are you holding up my friend?

JIMMY: [*makes a little sound and gives her a thumbs up*]

[*They all walk toward the side plane door to board. LAURIE has never been on such a plane before. She timidly walks inside and sees this is not a normal plane. She looks all around for the typical passenger jet feel of seats facing forward and where she can store her bag. The plane's engine starts and LAURIE gets scared as she feels the vibrations. She starts to grab on to something. She follows J.J. then J.J. points to seats where LAURIE and JIMMY will sit. There are only four facing the front.*]

J.J.: Get settled in, it's going to be about a ten-hour flight.

LAURIE: Ummm, what?

This is not a regular plane.

Where's the stewardess?

Why are all the seats so uncomfortable looking?

Ten hours?

SCENE 17

Where are we going?

J.J.: We are going to Malta.

LAURIE: Malta?

Where's that?

You never told me we were going overseas!

J.J.: You told me you would do anything to stop this scumbag from victimizing another person; that is where he is!

That is why I told you to take your passport.

LAURIE: [*with easygoing tone*]

Okay wake me up when they start serving food.

J.J.: [*with annoyed, harsh tone, and attitude*]

This is not a vacation!

Nobody is serving food, a hot towel, and there will be no

in-flight movie! We are going to get in and get out.

LAURIE: [*sounding shocked*]

Oh!? Oh yeah, I forgot…

You see I haven't been on a vacation in a long time, can't we just pretend?

FRIED CATFISH

J.J.: [*shaking her head talking to herself*]

I don't think this plan is gonna work.

LAURIE: Can't you just give me a drink?

To relax me after that crazy ride?

J.J.: [*just to appease LAURIE*]

Okay sure, you want a drink, I'll get you one.

[J.J. *walks to an area in the back of the plane. There is an area on the plane to get food/drink items. LAURIE doesn't see what she is doing. J.J. grabs a pill bottle from the cabinet and puts a sleeping pill in a cup with coke and a splash of rum to make her think it's a real drink, hoping it will relax her. She walks back to LAURIE with the drink and hands it to her. LAURIE is already buckled in.*]

J.J.: [*with sweet tone*]

Okay, here you go, this is all we have.

LAURIE: [*surprised tone in her voice that J.J. is being so nice*]

Why thank you J.J.!

[LAURIE *takes a sip, then drinks the entire glass in one big gulp. She hands the cup back to J.J.*]

LAURIE: [*relaxed tone in her voice*]

Ahh! That was good!

SCENE 17

[LAURIE *takes a small pillow she brought with her from her bag and places it behind her neck. She also has an eye mask and puts that on her eyes. JIMMY sees her and puts his hands over his eyes. LAURIE then turns her head sideways toward the window, falls asleep immediately and begins to snore. JIMMY then covers his ears.*]

[*J.J. goes to her seat, buckles up. Grabs her huge laptop and opens it. Puts in her earphones which are connected to the laptop.*]

[*The plane door closes—engines start revving up.*]

PILOT: [*over speaker*]

Ready for take-off.

[*Plane starts moving down the runway and takes off. While in flight we see J.J. on her laptop—she is typing—she pulls up the real picture of STEFAN and his name comes up as "Abel Bajada." A long list of crimes comes up near his name. The next picture she pulls up is the actual villain—his real name is: LEONARDO BIAGIO. She has reviewed his profile in the past.*]

J.J.: [SOFTLY TO HERSELF] We got you now Leo, we got you now.

[*She moves to the next window with what looks like a flight plan pinpointing a signal that shows Malta. She zooms in and it's a satellite which brings live video of the actual office location of where Abel is sitting. She screenshots it. J.J. spends most of her time during the flight confirming the current movements of LEONARDO BIAGIO.*]

END SCENE

SCENE 18

LEONARDO BIAGIO AT NIGHTCLUB

[LEONARDO BIAGIO *is in his house putting on his cufflinks, fixing his hair, checking his watch. He speaks into his watch, notifying one of his staff to get his car ready for him. He walks down an enormous marble staircase and goes to the front door. A beautiful red convertible sports car is waiting for him and a servant has the door open for him, waiting for him to enter. The servant closes the door and wishes him a good evening and he speeds off into the dark clear night. He drives down the hills from his home.*

He reaches the nightclub. A valet is waiting for him. He exits the car and walks toward the club door where a bouncer is talking to his watch. The bouncer lets him in.]

INT—CLUB—LOUD MUSIC—
CLUB IS FULL OF PEOPLE DANCING

[*A club concierge greets* LEONARDO *at the door and welcomes him in. The concierge then snaps his fingers, signaling two tall elegant/sexy looking women to approach* LEONARDO *from each side, each grabbing one arm. They proceed down a short staircase to the dance floor area; they walk by it and continue to a seating area near the bar. All three sit in a booth with* LEONARDO *in the middle. Drinks have already been ordered by the concierge and they are sitting on the table waiting for all three of them. No words are spoken. All three drink. The women start to put their arms on* LEONARDO *and kiss him, etc.*

SCENE 18

LEONARDO *gets bored and tells them to go dance.*

He then sees across the way; a well-dressed man who is sitting with a few people. This man is high up in the government of Malta. The man has a drink in his hand and raises his glass to LEONARDO. LEONARDO *returns the gesture by doing the same.*

Next to the well-dressed man is a very sexy woman. She makes eye contact with LEONARDO. *The well-dressed man whispers something in her ear. She proceeds to get up and walk toward* LEONARDO. *He can't stop staring at her. As she approaches his table he gets up to greet her. He leans over to her and gives her a peck on her cheek. She puts her hand on the top of his shoulder and she leans in. She places a microchip on him without him realizing it.*

The woman is an agent working for J.J.'s team. Now they are able to track his every movement from this point.

The woman sits with him for a few minutes, rubbing his leg, whispering something to him. In the meantime, he is scanning the room unaware of what just happened. He thinks that she is interested in him and when he asks her to join him at his place, she refuses. He brushes it off and leaves the club.

LEONARDO *arrives at his house around 2:00 a.m.*]

HOUSE OF LEONARDO—2:00 A.M. MALTA TIME

[LEONARDO *is in his room, already in his silky pajamas. One of his servants already had a tray with milk and cookies waiting for him.*]

LEONARDO: [*sitting in his bed with his laptop open and eating his cookies and milk*]

This is the life!

[*while reading emails, checking business*]

This is what makes it all worthwhile! Women?!

Who needs them when I have all this!

[*He closes his laptop, shuts off the lights, and goes to sleep. In the dark, a light comes through the window and zooms in on the microchip on his suit jacket lying on a chair.*]

END SCENE

SCENE 19

RETURN TO PLANE SCENE

[*They have been flying for 9 hours. They are almost at the end of the flight. All this time, LAURIE has been sleeping.*

The view from the plane is mountains, then green patches of land start to appear.

J.J. enters the cockpit to discuss final logistics with the pilot.]

J.J.: [*standing behind the pilot's chair bending over, looking at the view*]

How long do we have to drop off?

PILOT: Forty-five minutes. You'd better get ready.

[J.J. *leaves the cockpit.*

Walking to where LAURIE is seated, she starts to tap LAURIE's cheek with the back of her hand to wake her up. J.J. is already geared up for departure.]

J.J.: [*tap, tap*]

Wake up, sleeping beauty!

[*tap, tap, tap*]

Wake up!

[LAURIE *doesn't respond. J.J. gives LAURIE a hard smack across the face.*]

LAURIE: [*groggy, in pain-holding her cheek*]

Ooowww!!

What the hell!?

[*The monkey JIMMY has been sitting quietly all this time in a seat next to LAURIE; he had taken her eye mask and placed it on his face—the mask is far too big. When he hears the conversation he lifts the sleep mask off his eyes and watches.*]

J.J.: I had to wake you up!

LAURIE: That's how you wake a person up?!

J.J.: We don't have much time, get up!

LAURIE: [*still groggy—holding the back of her head*]

Why? Is the plane landing?

J.J.: Noooo, it's not landing, we are jumping!

LAURIE: Jumping?!

[*starting to become more coherent*]

What the hell are you talking about?!

[*LAURIE begins to look down at her outfit and realizes she's not wearing the same clothes she entered the plane in.*
While LAURIE was sleeping, J.J. changed LAURIE'S clothes to ones resembling a man's black military outfit with boots.]

SCENE 19

LAURIE: [*freaking out—arms start flailing all over the place, trying to find the buckle to the seat*]

[*pointing at J.J., loudly*]

YOU'RE CRAZY! I KNEW IT!

MY MOM WARNED ME, BUT I DIDN'T LISTEN!

WHAT THE HELL AM I WEARING?

WHAT DID YOU DO TO ME?

YOU'RE IN ON IT!

YOU'RE SICK!

J.J.: [*shocked look on her face*]

In on what?

LAURIE: [*still freaking out and increasingly frantic*]

THE SCAM!

YOU ARE PART OF THE SCAM!

AND SOME CREEPY THING THAT INVOLVES WOMEN IN CATSUITS!

J.J.: [*still standing in front of LAURIE, shaking her head, begins talking to herself*]

I knew it; I knew I shouldn't have hitched my wagon to this woman! J.J. go with your gut.

[she starts punching her gut area]

Go with your gut!

Oh lord! Jesus! What have I done?!

[LAURIE *just sits there and starts crying!*]

LAURIE: [*crying hysterically*]

> Just… just drop me off at the nearest airport and I promise I won't tell anybody about you or this!

> Just let me live!

J.J.: [*gets closer to* LAURIE *and grabs ahold of her*]

> Listen up!

LAURIE: [*eyes closed, starts turning her head from side to side*]

> No! No! I don't want to die!

J.J.: [*smacks* LAURIE *in the face*]

> Laurie! Look at me!

LAURIE: [*with shock*] Ooouuuuwwwww!

> What the hell?

> You hit me again?!

SCENE 19

J.J.: [*loud, deep voice, points her finger at* LAURIE]

Laurie! Listen to me!

I am not a scammer! I am with the ACF!

I told you the truth when we started this!

Laurie, you are just coming off a long sleep,
I think those pills were too strong, sorry!

[*voice gets softer*] This mission has been
going on for years and we are finally gonna
get this guy!

Without you, this mission would not have
gotten this far! You need to trust me!

[LAURIE *starts to calm down a bit.*]

LAURIE: Pills, what pills? Oh, my head.

Okay. [*pause*] [*wiping tears*]

Okay. [*pause*] I guess I have no choice.

J.J.: [*with compassion, sits in the seat next to*
LAURIE]

Laurie, that's where you are wrong! You have
a choice! You always had a choice! But, the
choices you made led you to this moment.
Here! With me, trying to catch a scumbag!

Once this mission is over, I am going to get
you someone to talk to about what happened

here. It's not your fault Laurie! You were looking for love and got scammed! What you are doing now is helping a lot of people like you who are just victims!

I hope you realize how strong you are!

LAURIE: [*putting her head sideways and wiping her tears*]

Now why can't you say things like that all the time?!

J.J.: [*shaking her head*]

Then I wouldn't be good at my job!

[*An alarm goes off in the cabin. The PILOT's voice comes on.*]

PILOT: Fifteen minutes.

J.J.: [*getting up from her seat*]

Okay come on!

We really need to get ready!

LAURIE: [*starts to sound a little hysterical again*]

What? Are you serious?

I thought we were good here!

I thought you were joking about jumping!

J.J.: I don't joke about that!

Never!

[*Alarms are still blaring. The back cargo door opens and air starts flooding in. LAURIE stands up and begins to sway a bit.*]

LAURIE: [*putting her hand on her head and sounding scared*]

I'm not jumping out of this plane!

Oh my god!

J.J.: Well girl! You ain't got a choice, 'cause this plane ain't landing!

We are being dropped off!

[*J.J. unzips a large side pocket on her jumpsuit and motions to JIMMY to jump in. He does.*]

LAURIE: [*screams loudly as she sees the entire back of the plane is open, realizing this is real*]

You'll have to drag me kicking and screaming!

J.J.: Okay! If that's how you want it!

[*J.J. places her flight glasses over her eyes then talks into her arm band/phone.*
The plane is also carrying a large wooden crate which will be unloaded in the air by parachute and land in a specific location in Malta. The crate is small, but contains a motorcycle with side-

car, their disguises, and anything they need. At this point, the PILOT has pushed a button which releases the cargo, and it tumbles out of the back. We assume it lands where it's meant to. There are other ACF agents in Malta who will pick this up and have it ready for J.J. and LAURIE. LAURIE sees the cargo leave the plane.]

J.J.: [speaking to pilot in her wrist phone]

Turn up!

[This signals the PILOT to tilt the plane upward, hurling LAURIE toward J.J. and the open cargo area.
LAURIE screams as she falls toward the back opening. She ends up grabbing a strap on the inside of the plane on the side.]

LAURIE: [screams]

AHHHHH!!!

[J.J. very quickly attaches herself to LAURIE with a hook then starts to pry LAURIE's fingers off. LAURIE resists. The air current is so strong LAURIE'S face has the G-force look.]

LAURIE: OH MY GOD! AHHHH!!

[J.J. starts to push LAURIE from behind. LAURIE is still hanging on. J.J. then kicks the back of LAURIE's knees. LAURIE clumsily falls down tumbling forward out the back of the plane. J.J. immediately follows behind her.
They are all outside the plane free falling. LAURIE is screaming with arms and legs flapping.

SCENE 19

[JIMMY's face (wearing goggles he found in J.J.'s pocket) is poking out of J.J.'s side pocket. Gives a thumbs up.

J.J. gets closer to LAURIE as they are free falling. Their suits have Velcro which allows J.J. to press up against LAURIE's back and they are now joined as one mid-air. J.J. places goggles on LAURIE's head. LAURIE pulls them over her face. They continue to fall. LAURIE is panicking.

J.J. looks at her watch/phone then pulls the cord to the parachute. The force of the air pulls them up. At this point LAURIE starts to calm down a bit.]

J.J.: We are just coasting now… just enjoy the ride!

LAURIE: Easy for you to say! I can't see where I am going! And I think I peed myself!

[*LANDING SPOT: NEARBY THE LOCATION THE CARGO LANDED. It's an open field with ACF agents waiting for J.J. and LAURIE with a truck and a few cars.*]

END SCENE

SCENE 20

STREETS OF MALTA—MALTA TIME—APPROX 4:00 P.M.

THEY LANDED SUCCESSFULLY AND HAD TIME TO CHANGE CLOTHES IN AN UNKNOWN LOCATION. LAURIE IS NOW ON A STREET FIVE DOORS AWAY FROM THE OFFICE/"INTERNET CAFÉ" WHERE THE CATFISH WORKS.

[*She is disguised in a brightly colored muumuu and headdress and pushing a baby carriage. In the carriage is JIMMY wrapped up/covered like a baby. He has in his hands what looks like baby toys on a ring shaped like bananas.*

LAURIE arrives at the location. They confirmed STEFAN is working now. J.J. is watching her from a distance and they are both equipped with tiny microphones to communicate. LAURIE can hear and speak to J.J. from the earpiece.]

J.J.: Okay, now act natural, blend in.

LAURIE: [*speaking softly and with attitude*]

Blend in? To what?

I look like a freak! Nobody is dressed like me; did someone get the wrong country?

J.J.: Stop complaining, that's all we could get in your size on such short notice. Now, make it work!

Make sure to pick up your baby!

SCENE 20

LAURIE: [*muttering under her breath, then takes a big deep breath and pushes the carriage to the door*]

[JIMMY *is lying in the baby carriage, sucking on his thumb. Then he shows his teeth in a laughing manner.*]

LAURIE: [*talking to* JIMMY] Oh, so you're an actor now? I'm sure you will be nominated for an academy award.

[LAURIE *arrives at the door of the office/internet café. The entire storefront-type office is all glass. There are rows of young men and women sitting there, approximately 30 workers. No one gets up to assist her. She struggles trying to open the door and push the carriage through. She tries on her own several times. The scammers inside stare at her and some look at each other, some laughing. She finally makes it in. JIMMY is covered up at this point. There's a small office space inside.*]

J.J.: [*talking through the earpiece*]

Now was that necessary?

You should not be attracting attention.

LAURIE: [*with a sheepish smile, gritting her teeth—she speaks softly*]

Next time, you try it!

[LAURIE *gets to the front counter which is reception; the others are in the next rooms (all glass). The* RECEPTIONIST *looks at her strangely and speaks.*]

RECEPTIONIST: [*speaks in French*]

　　May I help you?

LAURIE: [*a bit disheveled says in English*]

　　Ugh, yes, where's Stefan?

　　I am his wife, and the baby wants to see him.

　　[*looking down at* JIMMY *wrapped up*]

RECEPTIONIST: [*with questioning look on her face speaks English with accent*]

　　Stefan? There is no Stefan here.

LAURIE: [*loudly*]

　　WHAT?!

　　WHAT DO YOU MEAN MY HUSBAND IS NOT HERE?! WHERE IS HE?

　　IS HE CHEATING ON ME AGAIN?!

　　[*bangs on the counter*]

[*Knowing ahead of time that* LAURIE *might need help,* J.J. *from her position outside sends a text message to* STEFAN *to get him to call* LAURIE'S *phone to expose him. Even though they know what he looks like, they need him to stand out from the employees working there. LAURIE's reactions cause the workers to look at her and some become scared. The OFFICE MANAGER rushes to the reception desk after hearing a ruckus, but not what was said.*

The OFFICE MANAGER from the opening scene comes from the back office, stands in front of LAURIE.]

OFFICE MANAGER: [*with accent*]

May I help you madam?

LAURIE: Yes, who are you?

OFFICE MANAGER: I am the office manager.

LAURIE: Oh, well, then you must know my husband, Stefan!

OFFICE MANAGER: [*sternly*]

Madam, there is no one here by that name, you should go. [*motions for LAURIE to leave*]

[At that moment, LAURIE's phone rings, she sees it's STEFAN.

OFFICE MANAGER has puzzled look on her face.]

LAURIE: [*answers the phone*]

[*loudly*]

OH, STEFAN! THANK GOD! I'M HERE, I NEED TO SEE YOU!

ABEL/STEFAN: Oh, baby! I miss you! Where have you been? I kiss you.

[*starts making kissing noises*]

[OFFICE MANAGER *continues standing there, her arms folded.*

LAURIE *spots a young man making kissy faces into the phone sitting in the last row of the office part of the building.*

*In slow motion—*LAURIE's *face becomes angry and her eyes narrow—she zeroes in on* STEFAN.]

LAURIE: [*Slow motion: mouth hanging open—she mouths: "you asshole!"*]

STEFAN/ABEL: [*locking eyes with* LAURIE, *freezes*]

[*In slow motion mouthing oh shit"*]

[*Action ensues:*

LAURIE *pushes the baby carriage into the* OFFICE MANAGER. JIMMY *pops out of the carriage holding a key ring of tiny bananas which are actually small bombs.*

OFFICE MANAGER *falls to the floor.*

LAURIE *makes her way to the glass door, opening it, and rushes in.* JIMMY *follows her into the office where they are all sitting.*

The majority of the workers all get up. Everyone scatters; they rush around, trying to get out. JIMMY *takes a banana bomb and throws it in the air. It explodes, smoke fills one area.*

LAURIE *rushes over to where* STEFAN *is sitting. She confronts him.* STEFAN *is still seated in shock.*]

LAURIE: [*holding a banana bomb, pointing it at* STEFAN/ABEL's *face, speaks to* J.J.]

SCENE 20

I got him!

J.J.: Good job Laurie! I'm coming!

[LAURIE *takes the banana bomb and puts it on* STEFAN/ABEL*'s lap.*]

LAURIE: [*snarling look on face, gritted teeth*]

Go ahead Stefan, or whatever your name is, make a move, and little Stefan gets it!

[STEFAN/ABEL *is speechless, mouth hanging open. Doesn't move.*]

LAURIE: What's the matter Stefan or Abel, whatever your name is, you don't know what to say, *baby?*

[LAURIE *has a baby pacifier and shoves it in his mouth. His eyes widen. He's frozen in his spot.*
LAURIE *tells* JIMMY *to start pulling out the computer plugs; he starts making his way through the office unplugging computers, and scaring some workers.* LAURIE *turns back to the door, finds her way to the computer room. She takes a hammer from her headdress and starts smashing some of the hardware, takes a few banana bombs and throws them at the servers while she is making her way out of the room and back to the front to meet up with* J.J.]

FRIED CATFISH

MINUTES AFTER THE ACTION SCENE—OUTSIDE—OFFICE

[LEONARDO, *not knowing anything just happened in the office, drives in his sports car convertible to the office, parks outside. He has a briefcase on the passenger floor with a laptop computer in it. He leans over to pick it up, then notices all the workers running out in different directions. STEFAN/ABEL is sitting frozen with a pacifier in his mouth. Smoke filled in parts of the room. Sparks come from some computers.*

LEONARDO *calls the office number from his car, afraid to go inside, gets no dial tone. Still in his car he stands up in the convertible, looking inside, and sees his* OFFICE MANAGER *face down.*]

LEONARDO: [*holding his hand over his mouth screams like a girl*]

Ahhh!

[J.J. *is driving—we don't see in what until she pulls up to the office.*]

J.J.: Laurie, are you there girl?!

LAURIE: [*speaking loudly, out of breath as she walks from the computer room to the front door*]

Yes, what now?

J.J.: [*sternly*]

I spotted him, I got 'em in my sights, he's outside the office in the red convertible sports car.

SCENE 20

Meet me outside and I will pick you up!

[LAURIE *comes running to the front,* JIMMY *sees her and jumps on her back holding on to her neck.*]

JIMMY: [*turns to* STEFAN *and grits his teeth, gives him the middle finger*]

[LEONARDO *is scared to get out of his car; he sees* LAURIE *with* JIMMY *running to the door.* LAURIE *gets outside and stops to breathe.* LEONARDO*'s and* LAURIE*'s eyes lock.*]

LEONARDO: [*screams like a little girl*]

ARGH! *HELP!*

[LEONARDO *quickly sits back down in his car.* LAURIE *is about to jump in the passenger seat; he puts the car in drive and starts moving.* LAURIE *can't jump in, so she lets go of the door.* JIMMY *gets flung into the back of the convertible.* LEONARDO *speeds away not noticing that* JIMMY *is in his car.* LAURIE *is on the ground.* J.J. *pulls up with motorcycle and sidecar.*]

J.J.: [*looking down at* LAURIE]

Girl! You have to learn some skills!

LAURIE: [*screams*]

SHUT UP!

[*gets up and looks at what* J.J. *just pulled up in*]

J.J.: [*emphatically*]

Get in! We're losing him.

[LAURIE *unwillingly gets in the sidecar.* J.J. *throws a pair of black motorcycle goggles at* LAURIE. LAURIE *puts them on. They speed off to catch up with* LEONARDO.]

END SCENE

SCENE 21

CHASE SCENE—LEONARDO GETS CAUGHT

THROUGH THE STREETS OF MALTA, SOME STREETS ARE NARROW AND WINDING.

[JIMMY *jumps on* LEONARDO's *neck while he's driving; he then puts his hands over* LEONARDO's *eyes.* LEONARDO *screams and loses control of the car. Chase scene ends with* LEONARDO's *car taking flight and landing in a swimming pool in someone's backyard.*]

SWIMMING POOL, CAR FLOATING, LEONARDO INSIDE.

[JIMMY *jumps out and swims to the edge of the pool.* LEONARDO *can't swim, he screams.* J.J. *and* LAURIE *at this point are near the pool.*

J.J. *points a gun toward* LEONARDO, *with* LAURIE *making sure that* JIMMY *is okay.*]

J.J.: [*stern tone*]

Okay scum sucker, we got you!

LAURIE: Jimmy! You did a great job buddy!

J.J.: [*turning to* LAURIE]

Not now Laurie! Jimmy's a professional!

LAURIE: [*disgusted tone*]

Okay! Okay!

Geez, just giving him some praise!

J.J.: [*turns back to* LEONARDO*, deep voice*]

You are gonna transfer all the money you stole from this woman into her account!

LEONARDO: [*shrill voice*]

What money? Who are you? What do you want from me?

J.J.: [*scary look on her face*]

We are your worst nightmare come true!

You have stolen this woman's money with your fake profiles, your fake words, you demolish people!

Now you are gonna feel the wrath of what you've done to thousands of women, and men!

You scum sucking piece of shit!

LEONARDO: [*sounding scared*]

What? I don't even know her!

I don't know you, I am a businessman. I run a small business selling office products.

J.J.: [*emphatically*]

Yeah! You sell stuff alright!

You sell fake love and promises to unsuspecting gullible people who think they are gonna fall in love with a picture and some nice words that they have been wanting to hear their entire lives!

[*Upon hearing the word "gullible" LAURIE reacts.*]

LAURIE: [sounding hurt]

Hey, I'm not gullible! I believe in love!

J.J.: Leonardo Biagio!

We have been tracking you for years, you are a major scammer who started off in your parents' basement scamming innocent people out of their hard-earned money.

We know all about you and there is no turning back!

Leonardo knows he's been caught.

LEONARDO: [*trying to sound sincere*]

We'll, ugh, I never meant to hurt anybody. I thought I was doing them a favor. If they want to live in a fantasy thinking someone from a computer that looks much younger than them finds them attractive and loves what is being said to them, who am I to judge?!

[*smirking*]

They deserve to be scammed!

[*Both J.J. and LAURIE look at him with anger and sour expressions.*]

113

FRIED CATFISH

LEONARDO: [*shrugging shoulders*]

When I was 17, I had a stutter.

I wasn't the best looking guy either, look at me!

I've never found love and it doesn't bother me!

I'm rich now, women want to be with me!

LAURIE: [*with anger in her voice*]

Yeah, they want to be with you alright, only if you pay them. You pimp!

[*shaking her head*]

I can't believe there are people like you in this world who could destroy something so pure and innocent like love, and turn it into a nightmare!

I have lost everything because of you!

I am financially ruined and you just sit there in your expensive car and think it's okay?! Well, buddy, welcome to reality!

J.J.: [*sternly and pointing gun*]

Okay, enough of this chitchat! Get that laptop out, throw it to me!

[*The car is still somewhat floating, some water has gotten in.*

SCENE 21

LEONARDO *slowly grabs the briefcase, worried about the water, then tosses it out of the car. It floats and* LAURIE *gets on her knees to grab it from the pool.* LAURIE *takes it and gives it to* J.J. J.J. *turns to* LAURIE, *hands her the gun, takes the briefcase.*]

J.J.: [*to* LAURIE]

Now be careful with that!

[J.J. *opens the laptop, starts typing very fast, puts her flash drive into the laptop.*
The windows open and shut rapidly, being uploaded to flash drive. Screen now gets to a bank login page. It has everything except the password.]

J.J.: [*sternly, to* LEONARDO]

Now, give me your password!

LEONARDO: [*with childish/sarcastic voice*]

Make me!

LAURIE: [*angrily, pointing gun*]

Oh, we'll make you!

[LAURIE *accidently shoots the gun and pops one of the car's front tires. The car starts to tilt upward on one side only.* LEONARDO *screams loudly!*]

LEONARDO: [FRIGHTENED]

Don't shoot!

LAURIE: [YELLS]

GIVE US THE PASSWORD!

LEONARDO: [*frightened but adamant*]

No!

J.J.: [*sternly, to* LAURIE]

Shoot the other tire!

LEONARDO: [*now really scared*]

No! No! I can't swim!

LAURIE: [*yells*]

THEN GIVE US THE PASSWORD!

[LAURIE *at this moment has moved to the other side of the car, pointing the gun at the opposite tire.*
As if in slow motion, a single bullet fires out the barrel of the gun. Smoke comes out, camera goes to JIMMY's *face at the side of the pool and he has his hands over his face.*]

LEONARDO: [*screams out the password, camera in slow motion, he mouths in slow motion*]

E v o l!

[J.J.'s *hands type the word out on the laptop in the bank login screen. The screen opens, all the funds from his bank account transfer to the bank account which* J.J. *has set up. It's over 3 billion dollars.*]

J.J.: [*with happy tone*]

Gotcha!

[*shaking her head*]

Wow! You are evil! Your password is "love" spelled backwards!

[LAURIE *just stares at J.J. and sheds a tear.*]

[*Scene ends with* LEONARDO *being dragged from the pool like a drowned rat. J.J. and LAURIE don't speak, they just look at each other with huge smiles on their faces and embrace. A few other ACF agents come on the scene along with local police who have been made aware of the situation.*]

END SCENE

SCENE 22

FINAL SCENE

[*Eight months have passed since* LEONARDO BIAGIO *was caught.* LAURIE *has since joined the ACF. They have a new office where* LAURIE *lives in Wisconsin. We find* LAURIE *sitting at a desk typing into a large computer with two screens.* J.J. *walks in to her large office and sits down on the other side. Both are dressed up like businesswomen.*]

J.J.: Well Laurie, where's our next pick-up?

LAURIE: Rio de Janeiro.

THE END

About the Author

M.C., a Rhode Island native, new writer who has always loved comedy and superheroes from a very young age. Inspired by her Mom to laugh and enjoy good humor, she always loved watching movies and sitcoms and has a great imagination. In her early thirties, after a painful divorce, she found herself having to use dating websites to meet possible suitors rather than the old-fashioned way. She watched a few episodes of the *Dr. Phil* show of men and women being "Catfished", she learned the signs to watch out for and even caught a few herself before anything could happen. Today she is pursuing her dream of being a published writer and screenwriter.

She hopes this book is a eye-opener to people who may be in a similar situation, brings some sense of humor (though this is not funny), and the hope that justice can be served to those who are scammed.

Made in the USA
Middletown, DE
10 March 2021

34494899R00070